As she eased back against the sofa, Sara took the time to survey the sexy stranger.

A man like that wanted to be looked at. He took great care in his appearance and had to know he looked drop-dead sexy.

"Do you practice that look in the mirror?" he asked.

"What look is that?"

He stretched his arm along the sofa and behind her back as he eased a little closer.

"The seductive stare."

"Is that the look I'm giving?" she asked.

"Oh, I think you know exactly what you're doing," he told her, leaning just a bit closer. "The question is, what would you do if I took you up on that offer?"

* * *

Snowed In Secrets by Jules Bennett
is part of the Angel's Share series.

Dear Reader,

Welcome to the third and final book in my Angel's Share series! Are you ready for Sara and Ian? As I'm sure you've read, Sara is the lover of all things fairy tale, and I am so thrilled to bring you her story. I hope you love a good snowy trope as much as I do. This was definitely a fun one to write!

And who doesn't love a good Christmas story? What better time to fall in love than during the beauty of the holiday season. There's something so peaceful and magical about this time of year. Sara and Ian certainly have some obstacles to overcome, and they each have to deal with their pasts before they can look toward their future.

If you missed the first two books in the series, you can definitely read this one alone, but why would you want to? Go back and grab *When the Lights Go Out...* and *Second Chance Vows* to catch up on Sara's sisters and this dynamic trio.

Happy reading!

Jules

JULES BENNETT

SNOWED IN SECRETS

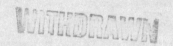

HARLEQUIN
DESIRE

HARLEQUIN®
DESIRE™

Recycling programs
for this product may
not exist in your area.

ISBN-13: 978-1-335-58147-1

Snowed In Secrets

For questions and comments about the quality of this book,
please contact us at CustomerService@Harlequin.com.

Harlequin Enterprises ULC
22 Adelaide St. West, 41st Floor
Toronto, Ontario M5H 4E3, Canada
www.Harlequin.com

Printed in U.S.A.

USA TODAY bestselling author **Jules Bennett** has published over sixty books and never tires of writing happy endings. Writing strong heroines and alpha heroes is Jules's favorite way to spend her workdays. Jules hosts weekly contests on her Facebook fan page and loves chatting with readers on Twitter, Facebook and via email through her website. Stay up-to-date by signing up for her newsletter at julesbennett.com.

Books by Jules Bennett

Harlequin Desire

The Rancher's Heirs

Twin Secrets
Claimed by the Rancher
Taming the Texan
A Texan for Christmas

Lockwood Lightning

An Unexpected Scandal
Scandalous Reunion
Scandalous Engagement

Angel's Share

When the Lights Go Out...
Second Chance Vows
Snowed In Secrets

Visit her Author Profile page at Harlequin.com, or julesbennett.com, for more titles.

You can also find Jules Bennett on Facebook, along with other Harlequin Desire authors, at Facebook.com/harlequindesireauthors!

For my girls, Grace and Madelyn.
Thank you for teaching me the true meaning
of unconditional love.

One

"Hey, Merle."

Sara Hawthorne greeted the owner of the Quiet Distil with a hug, then eased back, offering the elderly widower a smile. Not all of Angel's Share's clients were close like Merle Allen. But he'd been a loyal customer from day one and was more like a friend than a customer.

When Sara and her two sisters, Delilah and Elise, had started their distillery years ago, Merle had been one of their biggest cheerleaders. He'd told them as soon as they open that inaugural ten-year barrel of bourbon, he wanted first dibs. Sara liked to pop into his bourbon bar every few weeks to visit and just unwind.

And it was the desperate need for unwinding she searched for now. Between the holidays and her personal life, she had to find a few minutes just to herself.

"How's my favorite distiller?" Merle asked as he rested his hand on the glossy mahogany bar.

"I think you say that to my sisters, too." She laughed, leaning against the end of the bar top.

Merle shrugged. "You're all my favorite, what can I say?" His bright blue eyes crinkled around the edges as he chuckled, then pointed toward one of the VIP lounge areas. "Why don't you go on in and have a seat? I'll bring you something to take your mind off your troubles."

Sara tipped her head. "What makes you think I have troubles?"

He smiled as he shook his head and turned to move in behind the counter. "I own a bar. I know heartache when I see it. Now go on and settle in."

Since Sara figured Merle was rather experienced in recognizing a wounded heart, she obeyed. Per usual, she headed toward her favorite lounge area located all the way in the back of the bourbon bar.

Merle had been smart with the way he approached the interior of this place. Each of the rooms was different in motif and decor, but she always loved the cozy warmth of the White Dog Room. White Dog referred to the term of bourbon before it aged, but all of the rooms at the Quiet Distil had appropriate terminology-themed spaces and ambiance that catered to both male and female customers.

As Sara made her way toward the back of the bar, she passed the Rye and Mash Rooms. Both of those were nearly full with couples or friend groups laughing and enjoying their spirits. Another pang hit Sara as she continued down the wide hallway flanked with warm lighting made to resemble old gas lanterns.

On the skirts of pain in her heart came a healthy dose of guilt. She was happy for her sisters— thrilled, actually. They'd each found the love and happiness of their lives. Elise was off on her tropical honeymoon in Fiji with Antonio and Delilah had reunited with Camden after they'd teetered on the brink of divorce.

The ache Sara had lived with for too long threatened to turn her into a green-eyed monster. There was no need to be upset or jealous, that had never been in her nature anyway. Sara knew her time would come to find love, she was sure of it. And waiting for that proverbial knight in shining armor would be worth the time and energy she put into daydreaming…she hoped. Not that she ever needed anyone to save her, but she wouldn't mind a shoulder to lean on every now and again.

She wanted to hold hands in the car, snuggle on the couch after working all day, and talk about absolutely nothing and everything. She wanted forehead kisses and random "I love you" texts in the middle of the day.

Sara slid open the old oak doors and figured the White Dog Room would be just as crowded as the others, but there was only one couple occupying one of the tufted white leather sofas, so she would have a little privacy after all.

Perfect. She just wanted to gather her thoughts and take a little break from life. There had been a whirlwind to get Elise and Antonio married at the castle and Sara was so pleased with how everything turned out for their special day.

Angel's Share's wedding venue was officially open and another chapter in their business venture could be checked off. They were moving ahead through so many layers within their business and excelling at each one.

Angel's Share Distillery started twelve years ago in an old abandoned castle nestled in the hills of Benton Springs, Kentucky. The sisters had loved that unique place from the start and knew buying the historical property would set them apart from other distilleries. Not to mention, theirs was the only female-owned distillery in the country. Anything they could do to get a leg up on their competitors, they had to do. Standing out in this male-dominated field was a must for them to continue their success.

Sara turned toward the opposite side of the room and moved to the back. It was then that her breath caught in her throat and her knees grew weak.

She'd never experienced such a bold flash of lust in all of her life. But the man on the sofa nearly stole her breath. She certainly hadn't seen him at first glance, though she had no clue how she could have missed such a striking guy. The dark hair, the shadowy beard, black dress pants, crisp white shirt and black vest. He might as well have just popped out of a 1930s movie set. There was something to be said about a classy man who exuded confidence and elegance.

Mercy sakes, she blinked and glanced away for fear that she'd get caught staring. Surely a man who looked like that constantly got ogled and she wasn't the first. Also a man who looked like that wouldn't be in a bourbon bar on a Saturday night all alone. Likely his date had gone to the restroom, so Sara wasn't going to go anywhere near that section, either. Which left her options toward the front of the room.

"I thought I'd find you in your favorite place."

She turned to see Merle with a small charcuterie board of cheeses and fruit and nuts, plus a paddle with four different tumblers. He knew she loved the simplicity of the White Dog Room and she'd actually never even ventured into the others on her visits. She couldn't help but smile as she started to take the items from his grasp.

"No, ma'am." He shook his head and took a step back. "You tell me where you want to sit and I'll take it there."

Sara glanced around the spacious room, her eyes

immediately catching the sexy stranger in the corner. His mouth lifted in a smirk and she had a rush of arousal she certainly hadn't expected. Well, well, well.

Lust was one thing, but that curl of desire was on an entirely different level.

He held her gaze and continued to charm her with only a grin. Sara had to believe there was no date in the restroom. How was this guy all alone?

The way he stared back at her as he came to his feet had Sara squaring her shoulders and ignoring any nervous twinges.

"What about over there?" she asked Merle, pointing to the sofa the stranger sat on.

"Oh, do you know him?" Merle asked.

No, but I'm about to.

The intriguing stranger closed the distance between them and turned his attention to Merle.

"Could I get another Angel's Share ten-year?" he asked.

Oh, not only did he partake of her distillery bourbon, he had a voice smooth as whiskey to go with the mysterious exterior—as if she needed more reasons to be drawn to him.

"Of course, sir."

"I'll take this," Sara said, reaching for the charcuterie board. "Thanks, Merle."

"You let me know if you need anything else." Merle tipped his head in a nod and went to check on the couple on the opposite side of the room.

Sara shifted her focus back to the stranger and offered a smile. "Care to share this board with me?" she asked.

The guy's brows shot up and he shrugged. "It does seem like a good bit of food."

"Merle is a sweetheart," she explained. "He's always feeding me when I come in."

The striking man turned and headed back to the sofa he'd just left. Once the board and the sample drinks were on the honey-colored table, the stranger took his cell that had been on the sofa and slid it into his pocket.

"Have a seat." He gestured to the area right beside where he'd been sitting. "I take it you know the owner well?"

Sara took a seat, but left some space between them. He might be sexy and had piqued her interest, but he was still a stranger. Besides, as much as she wanted to find her happily-ever-after, she didn't think that would be in a bar and she sure as hell didn't want to come off as desperate.

"You could say that," she replied, then extended her hand in greeting. "My name is Jane."

At the last second she decided to use her middle name instead. In case he turned out to be weird, she didn't want him knowing who she really was.

He smiled, then reached for her hand and slid his thumb over her knuckles. He held on to her hand as he continued to keep his eyes locked on hers.

"You can call me Parker."

Sara eased her hand from his before she got lost in that deep voice, those dark eyes and that firm grip that made her wonder if he was as powerful as he appeared. What would a man like this do for a living? Traveling and dressed nice with shoes that had those classic red bottoms. Real estate? Architect? Definitely some type of business, but what?

She tipped her head and narrowed her eyes. "Parker is not your real name."

"Maybe, maybe not."

The mysterious man wanted to remain just that.

Unable to help herself, Sara smiled and found she actually enjoyed this odd meetup. Sounded sexy to her, but she still had to be cautious.

Another employee of the Quiet Distil came in carrying Parker's drink. Sara eased back onto the sofa, getting more comfortable with this situation. There was nothing to worry about. They were in a public place, they were having fun, and she was smiling and enjoying herself. What more could she ask for in an evening?

"Sir." The new hire sat the drink on the table and stepped back. "Is there anything else I can get either of you?"

Sara shook her head, her eyes still locked on Parker's and his on hers.

"We're good here," Parker stated without glancing up.

Once they were alone again, Sara reached for one of the samples Merle had given her. He always gave her different bourbons and whiskeys to try. Just because she was co-owner of Angel's Share, didn't mean she shouldn't stay abreast of her competition. It was good to see what else was out there and how her own company compared.

"So, what should we talk about? Careers? Favorite colors?" she asked, swirling the amber contents of her glass.

Parker laughed. "I'd rather know what you're doing here alone looking like you're carrying a whole host of problems."

For a virtual stranger to see something, Sara wondered what she must have looked like when she came in. She hadn't been surprised when Merle noticed because she was in here often enough and he knew her quite well. But this guy? Maybe he wasn't a businessman at all. Perhaps he was some sort of doctor or therapist.

Great. That would certainly kill any mood if a hunky guy tried to get into her head and decipher all of her past. She wouldn't put that on someone she'd just met.

"Do I look like I'm sad?" she asked, pasting on her sauciest smile, hoping to dodge the statement entirely.

"You look like you don't want to be," he countered.

Well, so much for that sassy grin and the dodge.

"Everyone has their secrets, and I'd like to keep mine close to my chest."

Parker nodded in agreement, or perhaps that was understanding. Either way, he shifted his focus to the contents of his glass as he gave a gentle swirl. She studied his dark, disheveled hair, those thick black brows and the fan of his heavy lashes. How did one person have so much sexuality and mysteriousness surrounding them?

She was glad she'd chosen to sit in this room and come over to his corner. Spending the evening alone hadn't necessarily appealed to her, but she also hadn't wanted to just stay home. Finding someone at the Quiet Distil was definitely an added perk to her day.

"You like bourbon?" he asked, his eyes darting back up to her.

"What's not to love?" she replied. "That little bit of smoky char, the smooth, rich flavor from the oak barrel, the way it warms you from the inside out."

"You seem to be quite the connoisseur." His crooked smile had the corners of his eyes crinkling, which only made him even sexier. "So what is it that you do?"

Sara lifted her snifter. "Drink bourbon. What about you?"

"Wait in bars for sexy women to come through."

"And does that usually work out well for you?"

Parker shrugged. "I'll let you know in a few hours."

Well, wasn't he a smooth one? Maybe that's why she found him so fascinating. Attractive, mysterious and clearly just as interested in her. A little flirting would be good for her. She hadn't had a date in a few months, and not that this was a date, but close enough. She hadn't really had time to find a date, let alone go on one.

A little banter, a little drinking…there was absolutely no harm and Sara believed this was exactly what she needed. With her sisters always with their significant others and not as free for social time as they used to be, Sara was clearly going to have to make her own fun and start her own traditions.

"I actually work in events," she told him, keeping her career super vague to keep up the element of mystery. "I make sure people have the time of their lives and then I get paid for it."

"Sounds like you love it."

"Nothing better," she agreed. "And my favorite color is white, you know, in case you want just a touch of personality."

Parker's dark brows drew in as he jerked back. "White? I've never met anyone who said white."

"You've never met anyone like me." She sipped her bourbon and offered a smile. "White is underrated, and it's the color of all the things I love. Most carbs, the wedding dress I have pictured in my head, the clouds when I daydream."

Parker laughed and shook his head. That burst of deep, robust laughter sent shivers through her. Flirty chatting was one thing, but the moment she started getting those giddy feelings, she really needed to dial it back a notch. She'd known this guy for all of twenty minutes. Just because he dressed well, had that whole dark vibe going on and smelled extremely sexy didn't mean anything was going to come from this encounter…though she wouldn't mind knowing how long he was in town for and maybe seeing him again.

Sara knew in her heart there was someone out there for her. She knew without a doubt that as soon as she saw "the one," she would be immediately swept off her feet and head over heels. She had all the clichés logged into her mind and was more than ready for that day to happen.

But until then, she'd just enjoy her time with chance encounters such as this one.

"Interesting take on your favorite color," he told her. "So, these events that you do, I assume you work with weddings since you said wedding dresses and you make people happy."

"I actually just finished working on a wedding."

Elise had made a beautiful bride and no matter that wedding planner wasn't Sara's job, she took that position very seriously when helping to pull off the big day for her sister. Sara had worked damn hard on that memorable event, and her spreadsheets and articulate planning had made the entire wedding come off without a hitch. Now she and her sisters were ready to start booking outside weddings and other venues. This was just another manner in which Angel's Share was set apart from so many other distilleries. Who wouldn't want to get married in an old historic castle?

Maybe one day for her…

"Yet you're single."

Parker's statement shifted her focus back to his intense gaze.

"How do you know I'm not married?" she asked.

He pointed to her hands. "You have jewelry on, yet nothing on your ring finger. You also don't seem like the type to leave a husband at home to come out to a bourbon bar and chat with random strangers."

"Maybe I just left that off my list of hobbies."

Once again, Parker laughed. "Touché."

"I actually hold marriage in high regard," she amended. "I'm not married, but when I do get married, I hope to still come out to amazing places like this, just with my husband."

"He will be a lucky man."

Sara sat her empty tumbler back in the empty slot on the tray and chose another.

"If he exists," she murmured.

As she eased back against the sofa with a new sample, she took the time to survey Parker once again, this time not caring one bit that he noticed. A man like that wanted to be looked at, he took great care in his appearance and had to know he looked drop-dead sexy.

"Do you practice that look in the mirror?" he asked.

"What look is that?"

Parker stretched his arm along the sofa and behind her back as he eased a little closer.

"The seductive stare."

"Is that the look I'm giving?" she asked.

"Oh, I think you know exactly what you're doing," he told her, leaning just a bit closer. "The question is, what would you do if I took you up on that offer?"

Two

What the hell was he doing? He didn't have time to entertain any extracurricular activities. He owed his editor a favor and once that was done, Ian Ford could actually start writing his novel. He'd saved enough money and made wise investments over the years to stay home and focus on his dream of writing his first book. Hopefully that would lead to more and spawn a new career.

Ian only had to be in Benton Springs, Kentucky, for two weeks, max. He'd do his interviews, conduct all the research needed to complete this piece, type it all out in silence and solitude, and then have everything wrapped up and turned in before the new year.

A perfect plan for the perfect ending to his illustrious career with *Elite*.

"Who says I'm offering?"

Jane's question pulled him back to the moment. Ian couldn't help but laugh.

"Maybe not with words, but that silent stare is more than inviting."

She lifted one slender shoulder, causing her silky black hair to slide around. Ian pressed his fingertips together, resisting the urge to reach out and see if those strands were as soft as they appeared. He'd been too damn long without a woman and in an instant this striking vixen had captured his attention in a way no one had done in years.

"I practiced the look in the car before I came in."

The way she continued to smirk in a sultry way with one brow tipped and her mouth in a soft grin, Ian wasn't quite sure if she was serious or not.

Regardless, he was a sucker. Damn it. He didn't come to town to be sidetracked by a seductive woman on day one. But turning away from her now would be impossible. She stirred a desire in him he sure as hell hadn't expected. This awakening wasn't something to be ignored.

She cocked her head, clearly waiting on a reply. Those strands brushed along his fingertips and another stir of arousal churned within. And here he thought he'd hate this trip to Kentucky in the dead of winter.

Ian didn't resist her again. He slid her strands

through his fingers, and yes, they were just as satiny as he'd imagined. Now his mind went to her full lips and wondered how long he'd be able to resist those.

"How long are you in town?" she asked.

Thrown by her question, Ian gathered his thoughts. "Not long. I assume you live here?"

"Best place in the entire world, especially at Christmastime."

He shifted even closer now as he continued to tease the strands of her hair between his fingers. Red flags waved all around inside his head, but he completely ignored them. He wanted more from her, not quite sure what yet. He also wasn't about to give up his anonymity…not for anybody.

"And have you traveled around the world?"

Jane smiled and there was no way to ignore another punch of desire to his gut. He couldn't figure out if she knew her potency and used it to cast men under her spell or if she was innocent and had no idea…but a woman who looked like every fantasy come to life couldn't be too innocent.

"Not much, but enough to know I belong here."

"You seem to know what you want."

Jane's eyes dropped to his mouth, then back up. Without a word, she reached for his tumbler on the table.

"I've always known what I wanted," she informed him, swirling the contents of his glass.

And she didn't mean his drink, if that heavy-lidded stare told him anything.

There was something extremely sexy about a bold woman, a woman who didn't play coy or bat her lashes and giggle. Not that he was looking for anything, but Jane was too intriguing and mysterious to simply ignore.

Some women who demanded attention were right up in your face, more than eager to talk about themselves. But Jane demanded attention in such a stealthy way that he found her absolutely refreshing. Her appearance, the way she held eye contact, the easy banter.

No, there was no way he could just get up and walk out. He would stay here as long as she did, and closing the place down didn't seem like such a bad idea right now.

Once the bourbon samples and the charcuterie board were gone, Ian still remained close as he listened to Jane discuss her favorite hangout spots in Benton Springs. All of them revolved around bourbon, which wasn't surprising. This part of the country took its spirits very seriously. Even nondrinkers enjoyed the atmosphere of the low-key bars and restaurants that were rich with the history of the rolling Kentucky hills. Ian almost wished he had more time to spend here, but two weeks was more than enough…especially with the threat of snow.

There was a reason he'd moved south to Miami. Winters in the north had destroyed his life and he'd vowed never to be here again. Yet here he was as a favor to a dear friend, but after this he would never subject himself to icy roads again.

Ian reached up and slid his finger along his scar just beneath the stubble along his jaw. The jagged skin was always the reminder of where he'd come from…and what he'd lost.

A chime sounded from her purse and Jane smiled as she reached around to dig in her bag. The intrusion was a welcome one because staying stuck in his head was a miserable place to be.

"Excuse me," she told him. "You never know when there's an emergency."

Ian studied the way her slender fingers slid over the screen, the little smile that danced around her mouth as she read the message. With a soft sigh, she slid the device into the side pocket and shifted back to face him.

"Sorry about that. I didn't realize it had gotten so late." She glanced around the room and laughed. "And now we're the only ones here. I didn't even see that other couple leave."

No, he hadn't, either, but he hadn't once thought about the time or anyone else in the bar. He also hadn't thought about work or the anxiety that had been eating at him coming back to the snowy north for the first time in twenty years.

"I'd say they're getting ready to close," she stated. "As much as I hate to go, I probably should head out."

She came to her feet and shifted her hair over

one shoulder before she reached down to grab her bag. Then those dark eyes landed on his once again and he knew he wasn't ready for their time to come to an end. He had not planned on the unforeseen events of this night, nor had he planned on what to do once they needed to leave.

"This has been a nice surprise," she told him.

Ian stood, leaving very little distance between them. Her eyes widened, but she didn't step back. She smiled after a beat and tipped her head.

Once again, Ian found himself reaching for her. This time, he trailed his fingertip along the side of her face, tucking her hair behind her ear, then gliding his hand on down her jawline. She didn't look away, didn't blink. He had her full attention.

"I'm usually not a fan of surprises," he murmured. "But I might just have to change my stance on that topic."

"I love them," she told him, her voice a little breathier than before.

"I'm not ready to end this night."

He hadn't meant to voice his thought, but the words slipped out and now hovered in the minuscule space between them. No regrets. That was something Ian never did, so now he would just see how the rest of the night played out.

"Who said this had to end?" she countered.

That desire churned in his gut once more, and he couldn't help but recognize the fact that he was spiraling completely out of control here and for the first time in his life, he didn't care. For a man who prided himself on never letting anyone or anything rule his emotions, he wasn't doing a very good job of holding on to that self-control. And while he wasn't about to completely lose himself here, he had to at least explore what the hell had him so intrigued and mesmerized.

"I rented a house for my visit if you'd like to continue the party there," he informed her. "We can stay out on the patio so you feel safe since I am a stranger."

Jane's smile widened. "I'll follow in my car."

Before Sara left the parking lot of the Quiet Distil, she fired off a text to Delilah telling her she was going to meet a guy for a drink and she'd send her location shortly. Just because the guy was sexy, fascinating and every girl's fantasy didn't mean she could be foolish. She still had to stay safe, and he'd reassured her they'd remain outside. The fact that he wanted her to feel safe only added to his charm.

Part of her wanted to know more, though. She wanted his real name, where he was from, all of the basic information. But he was just passing through and clearly wasn't looking for more.

Well, she was looking for more, but until the day came, she'd simply enjoy herself along the way. What other choice did she have? Wallow in misery? That wasn't in her makeup.

Just because she was the last woman standing in

regard to relationships in her family didn't mean she would grow to be some old lonely woman. Good things come to those who wait…right?

Sara really wanted to stop living by cheesy clichés and start making the most of her life the way she'd always envisioned it. Complaining wouldn't change anything, but she was human and on occasion she could be cranky.

Not tonight, though. How could anyone be in a bad mood when a charismatic stranger, who was more than easy on the eyes, gave such an inviting proposal? There was no denying the attraction and had she turned him down, she would have always wondered what she'd missed out on.

The fact that they weren't sharing personal details only made their impromptu meeting even more thrilling. She'd never been so mysterious with a man before and going by her middle name still kept her grounded, but she couldn't lie. Having the facade around her made her feel a little saucy, even a little flirtier than she'd ever been. She could be anyone she wanted tonight and right now, she was feeling more powerful and audacious than ever before.

Sara followed Parker's taillights as he made another turn down the snowy road. She rarely made it to this part of the county. Her home was on the other side, but lovely temporary rental homes were all over this area. People came from around the world to see the unique history nestled in these foothills and visit all of the distilleries. The distillery business had exploded over the last several years and the timing of her and her sisters' launching Angel's Share couldn't have been better.

For the moment, most things in her life were falling into place…save for the lack of a partner and the fact that she'd found out her adoptive mother was actually her biological aunt and her birth father was out there somewhere.

Sara blew out a sigh and pulled into the drive behind Parker. She was not about to let her personal life's issues ruin this moment. She still couldn't believe she'd followed a stranger to his home, but she fired off the location to Delilah, feeling safer already.

The two-story cottage with a wraparound porch seemed so quaint and almost…innocent. Seeing something so normal and average put this situation into a more realistic perspective. Flirting in a bar was one thing, but now, they would be alone and even though the promise of not going inside was made, that didn't mean things wouldn't progress. She'd never been one for a fling, but she wouldn't turn up her nose at one, either.

There was something so mystifying about Parker. He had been so gallant and self-assured without being a jerk. She hadn't dated jerks in the past, honestly, but nobody had ever really grabbed her attention for more than a few dates. And clearly she wasn't looking to date Parker, but she almost wished he'd be in town longer so they could explore this instant attraction. Something this fierce and powerful had never happened to her before.

Which was all the more reason to enjoy tonight… whatever may come her way.

She'd just set her cell back in her purse when her door opened. The dome light came on and she instantly turned to face her host as the cold blast hit her. He stood at the opening, looking down at her with a crooked grin that some might say was a little naughty and a whole lot cocky. She had a feeling she might get a better glimpse into the real Parker, but how much did he want to reveal? How much did she?

"Are you thinking about leaving?" he asked, resting one hand on the top of her car and the other on the open door.

"Not at all," she informed him. "I texted a couple people to let them know where I was in case you decide to get weird."

He stared for a moment before shaking his head and extending his hand.

"I will never understand what women go through with always worrying about safety measures."

She slid her hand into his as he assisted her from the car. That strong hold sent another round of tingles through her entire body. The building anticipation of what would happen during her visit also kept her stomach in knots—in the absolute best way, though. And the fact that he acknowledged her legitimate concern was definitely another check mark in his favor.

"If I didn't feel safe, I wouldn't be here," she said as she slid from her car. "But I still want to protect myself."

"Nothing will happen to you here."

The conviction in his tone made her feel secure in her decision to join him at his place. She definitely never would have invited him back to her place. At least this was neutral ground, since he was passing through.

Parker's fingertips trailed up her arm and back down as he laced his fingers with hers. She allowed him to lead her toward the path that led around to the back of the house. When he unlatched the gate, she hesitated for just a moment.

Parker's attention turned to her as he stopped as well. "The patio is beautiful with a nice view, and I promise we will be warm. I will leave this gate open, but if you'd rather sit on the front porch, that's fine, too. Just tell me where you're comfortable."

Why did he say all the right things? Clearly there was a woman in his life at some point who had taught him manners and morals. A mother? A sister? A special friend? There was so much she wanted to ask and explore with this man.

Sara offered a smile instead. "Lead the way. I'd love to see this view."

With her hand still firmly in his, he led her the rest of the way down the snow-covered path and around the back of the house. Sara gasped and stilled once more as she took in the beauty.

"I thought you might enjoy the ambiance out here," he told her.

Parker released her hand and stepped aside so she could take in the serenity of the property. The front of the home had been plain, but the back more than made up for that. A large porch, complete with a covered hot tub, a large garden area with benches and a pergola, and twinkling lights draped all over the place as if they had their own little stars shining just for them. Everything was covered in a fresh white blanket of snow, which only made the scenery seem somewhat magical.

"Let's head up to the porch," he told her. "It's freezing out here."

Sara laughed as he tugged her toward the steps, but then carefully held on to her so she didn't slip. Clearly he wasn't from around here, because she loved this weather. Yes, it might be cold, but in December what did he expect? She'd hate living somewhere where she decorated her home for Christmas wearing flip-flops. This was the weather she wanted for the holidays.

"I didn't expect such beauty back here," she told him as they reached the spacious covered patio.

Sara swiped the dampness of the snowflakes from her face and her hair, then sat her purse on the closest chair. When she focused once again on Parker, he was simply standing there staring down at her. Glistening flakes clung to his long, inky lashes and dotted white all over his dark hair. And that mouth.

His mouth seemed to just beg her to reach out and touch…so she did.

With her eyes locked firmly on his, Sara reached out and slid her thumb across his bottom lip. His eyes locked solely on her as the snow continued to whirl around, trapping them in some winter wonderland of beauty and romance.

But this wasn't romance. This was merely two strangers who weren't ready to end their night.

Just when she started to pull back, Parker reached up and gripped her wrist, holding her in place. With one step, he closed the distance between them.

"Is this when you kiss me?" she asked.

"This is when you kiss me," he corrected.

Three

Sara wasn't about to waste another moment, not when she'd been staring at that mouth all night. Lifting up onto her toes, she leaned in and slid her lips over his. Lightly at first, wanting to take in just a slight touch to get familiar with him.

But in an instant, Parker wrapped his arms around her waist and tugged her against his hard, strong body. Something snapped inside her as well as she thrust her fingers through his hair. The warmth of his body warded off any of the chill that surrounded them. Parker coaxed her lips apart and took the kiss to another level and she simply couldn't get enough. What had started as fun banter only hours ago had moved at a faster pace than she'd ever gone before.

Was this a mistake? Was this heated fling too good to be true?

No and no. She deserved a sliver of happiness, even if it was all temporary. With the shock of finding out her biological history, losing the only woman she'd known as a mother, and her sisters finding the loves of their lives, Sara couldn't help but feel alone lately.

While she wasn't one to have a self-pity party, she couldn't help herself right now. Parker was the perfect distraction for everything that weighed heavy. Besides, this was only for one night. What could be the harm in taking advantage of a perfectly delicious opportunity?

Softly, he nipped at her lips before easing back. He ran his hands up and down her arms.

"You're trembling."

Was she? She wasn't even cold—far from it.

Parker took a step back and turned away. "Give me a minute to light these heaters and it will be warm out here in no time."

She remained in place, still trying to process that kiss that seemed like it could be a stepping-stone to so much more. That kiss had been almost like a promise, like he wanted that next level but he'd been gentlemanly enough to not push.

Dee would be so appalled that she was here with a man she'd just met and moving so fast. She would tell her this wasn't safe, she'd tell her she shouldn't settle for a quickie. If Elise were here she'd think the same. That's why Sara didn't check to see if Dee had responded to her texts. It was easy for them to say, but she wasn't settling. She was enjoying herself while this stranger was in town and obviously he wanted to enjoy himself, too.

Parker propped his hands on his hips and stared at the heater near the outdoor seating area. He raked a hand over the back of his neck and shook his head. As he bent down, he cursed beneath his breath.

"Do you need help?" she offered.

"I've never seen a heater like this. It can't be that hard to figure out."

Sara made her way over, bent down beside him, turned the knob, clicked the ignite button and had a flame in seconds.

"It's not," she agreed.

He shot her a glance with one dark brow raised. "Show-off."

"Maybe," she said with a shrug.

She stood back up and held his gaze as he slowly rose, too. His dark stare never wavered and that energy she'd felt with him only moments ago seemed to just get stronger. How should she react to this? Tearing his clothes off seemed a little too forceful, but damn it. She had a need she couldn't explain.

"I can run inside and grab a couple of blankets," he suggested.

"That would be nice."

Sara took a seat on the sofa closest to the heater and curled deeper into her coat as Parker punched in a code on the panel to get into the house. At this point she didn't know if she was shivering from anticipation or arousal, but it wasn't the cold.

Moments later, he returned with a large comforter.

"All I could find was what was on the bed." He laughed. "Do you want a drink?"

"I'm good, but thanks."

The last thing she needed was a drink, because she didn't know how long she was staying. If she had more alcohol, she wouldn't be able to drive to leave and she didn't want to hinder her thoughts or actions, especially where Parker was concerned. So either way, she needed to remain nice and sober.

"When I found this place online, the large covered patio is what sold me." He took a seat next to her and spread the blanket out over both of them before shifting to face her. "A hot tub in the winter just seemed like the perfect way to relax."

"I've never had a hot tub." Sara tucked her hands beneath the comforter and adjusted so she could face him, too. "Have you been in this one yet?"

"Not yet. You up for it?"

Sara jerked back. "Is that why I'm here? A little skinny-dipping session?"

"You're here because you want to be here," he corrected, then shrugged. "Anything else is up to you."

Skinny-dipping in a hot tub with snow fluttering all around them was that level of romance she'd been wanting, even dreaming about. But there was no romance with a man she'd only known a few hours. That was quite a stretch of the imagination even for her.

"You're too tempting," she murmured.

The corners of his mouth kicked up in a grin she found all too thrilling and promising.

"I always welcome compliments."

Sara rolled her eyes. "I have a feeling you don't need help in the compliment department."

Something dark came over his face, she couldn't quite pinpoint it, but there was a sadness she hadn't seen before. In a flash, the pain vanished. Maybe she hadn't seen anything at all or perhaps he had his own demons he battled.

Regardless, she wasn't here to dig deeper into his life, just like she didn't need him looking further into hers.

"I've never been in a hot tub, nor have I ever been skinny-dipping," she admitted.

His eyes widened. "Never? You must have a grueling job if you don't make time for a little fun."

"I'm having fun now."

Parker stretched his arm along the back of the sofa and toyed with the ends of her hair just like he'd done back at the Quiet Distil. He seemed to be getting quite comfortable with her, which made her feel safe.

"You have a thing for my hair."

His eyes held hers. "I have a thing for you."

"Something we have in common."

His brows rose. "You have a thing for you, too?"

"You know what I mean," she joked.

He shifted once more and his hand brushed hers beneath the blanket. She thought he might lace their fingers together, but he flattened his palm on her thigh, which only sent another burst of heat through her. At this rate, she wouldn't need the blanket, the heater or the hot tub.

Though the mental image of the two of them naked in the bubbling water did nothing to squelch her rapidly growing desire. Had she seriously just met him only hours ago?

"Are you in town through Christmas?" she asked.

"No. I'm only here for two weeks, or less if I finish my job early."

"Any family to spend the holidays with?"

He cocked his head. "No personal questions, remember?"

She remembered, but she couldn't help herself.

"I've never done this before," she admitted. "I mean, I've talked to strangers and gotten to know them, but I've never kept everything so secretive. I'm not sure what to ask here."

"Who said we have to talk? Just enjoy the night."

Enjoying the night sounded so promising and intriguing.

"Do you like to travel?" she asked.

Parker's low laugh sent tingles through her. "You just can't help yourself, can you?"

Sara shrugged. "Not really."

He turned further into her, that hand on her thigh slid to her opposite hip as he shifted her more toward him. Sara stared up into his chocolate eyes, the glow from the heater and the porch lights reflecting all the amber flecks. The man was simply beautiful in both the dark and mysterious way and the charming, handsome sense. There had to be flaws, nobody was perfect, but she hadn't seen any yet and she wasn't about to start looking. She planned on enjoying the evening just like he'd told her to.

And since she didn't know what to talk about, she closed that distance between them and covered his lips with hers. Parker's grip on her hip tightened and he didn't disappoint in that kiss. He threaded his other hand through her hair and tugged softly, tipping her head back so he could have full access.

Damn, that man knew how to turn a kiss into a full-body experience.

With her hands still beneath the blanket, she reached for him. One hand on his chest and the other on his thigh. She wanted to touch, but didn't know what invisible line she should or shouldn't cross. They'd been dancing around the inevitable for hours. She wasn't naive about why she'd decided to come here. She had wanted him from that first glance and from his actions, there was no doubt he wanted the same thing.

This was absolutely drastic and completely out of character for her...which is what made this moment so much more thrilling. She wanted to be bold, she wanted to live her life in a more exciting way than ever before. If this past year had taught her anything, it was that she needed to always be in the moment.

Which was precisely what she was doing.

Sara slid her hand up over his shoulder and framed his jaw as she opened fully for him. His fingertips released their grip just enough to travel on up to the button of her coat. He had her coat undone in no time and eased back just enough to look down into her eyes.

He said nothing—he didn't have to. Sara kept her gaze locked onto his and shrugged out of her coat, letting it fall behind her.

"Please at least tell me you're not married or have someone waiting for you back home," she murmured.

"I have no family."

His statement hit that wounded spot in her heart, but she couldn't focus on his backstory now. That wasn't what this night was about.

"This is crazy," she whispered with a soft laugh.

Parker smoothed her hair back and framed her face with his hands. The way he looked at her as if he could read her every thought or see deep into her soul only captivated her even more.

"There's no pressure. Anything that happens or doesn't is up to you and fine with me."

"I said it was crazy, not that I wanted to stop."

Sara flattened her palms on his chest and eased him back until she was the one hovering over him.

Parker's eyes widened with excitement and arousal. Clearly she'd caught him off guard and apparently he didn't mind a dominant woman.

"Unless you want to stop." She lifted her knee onto the sofa and came up on it to lean even further over him. "I can go anytime."

Instantly his hands encircled her waist as he tugged her toward his chest.

"I like you right here."

Her lips were merely a breath away, so she kissed him again. She didn't recall enjoying kissing this much with anyone before. A kiss with Parker was definitely something to thoroughly relish and since this was all temporary, she wanted to get in as much as she could.

When his bare hands slid beneath the edge of her sweater, another round of shivers coursed through her, but this was so much more intense than any before. Having his skin against hers in an innocent yet intimate way put her desire on a whole other level.

Was all of this passion and desire stemming from the shadowy guise they were under? Or was there really some unexplainable, intriguing chemistry between them?

Sara rested her hands on his shoulders and let him explore her mouth and her body. She wanted rid of these clothes. She honestly couldn't even remember what bra and panties she had on because being with a man had been the last thing on her mind when she went out tonight.

Regardless, she didn't think her undergarments would hinder this union and she was tired of waiting for him to make the next move. Part of her was glad he was being so accommodating and making her feel safe, but she wished like hell he'd just jerk her clothes off.

Sara eased back and gripped the hem of her sweater. Slowly, she eased it up and over her head, tossing it to the side.

From the way Parker's eyes roamed over her chest and torso, the material of her bra was definitely a nonissue.

But that stare didn't last long. In the next moment there was a flurry of hands and clothes were flying. The blanket fell to the floor without a care along with their unwanted garments. The cool air hit her skin, but she didn't care. The warmth from the heater and Parker was all she needed.

In her haste to try to look somewhat sexy and remove everything, she hadn't realized Parker had procured protection until she saw him holding the package in one hand and tossing his wallet to the floor with the other.

Obviously something she should have been asking about, but now it was done and she didn't have to. At least one of them had their common sense about them.

His eyes locked onto hers and she stilled.

"Be sure," he told her.

Without a word, she took the foil pack and tore it

open. Once the protection was in place, she straddled his lap and rested her hands on his shoulders.
The second his gaze locked onto hers, she joined
their bodies and couldn't stop herself from moaning.
Sara stilled for just a second to take in the intensity
of the moment. She closed her eyes and dropped
her head back, welcoming each satiating emotion
to consume her.

Parker's hands slid up her bare thighs, over her
hips, and settled at the dip in her waist as he started
to move beneath her. Sara had no choice but to
match his rhythm.

"Look at me," he commanded.

That low, throaty demand had her refocusing
her attention on his face. The desire and fierce-
ness staring back at her sent another burst of arousal
spiraling through her. How could someone be so
powerful, yet so gentle at the same time?

Parker's hands came up to frame her face as he
pulled her mouth down to his. His pace quickened
the second his lips met hers. He consumed her completely. Her every thought, her every emotion. She'd
never had a man make her feel so out of control, yet
so powerful at the same time. He'd let her take the
lead, he'd waited on her to give any sign she wasn't
ready for this, but all the while he'd also made her
feel sexy, wanted, needed.

Parker reached around and fisted his hand in her
hair, giving it a slight tug. She pulled her lips from
his as he trailed his mouth down her neck and to the

swell of her breasts. If she thought she'd been plea-
sured before, that was nothing compared to what
Parker was doing to her now. His hands and mouth
seemed to be exploring her everywhere at once. She
wasn't opposed to her new lover's skills.

His hips pumped faster and she kept up the frantic pace. Her body seemed to curl from the inside
out with a need that took over and had her crying
out, digging her nails into his bare skin and resting
her forehead against his. The climax slammed into
her as fierce and fast as this man had come into her
life. She didn't care that she cried out or moaned.
There was no controlling her reactions or sensations.

Parker's grip tightened. Seconds later, his entire
body shook as the muscle in his jaw clenched. Sara
slowly came down off her high, just in time to ap-
preciate the view. For the first time since she'd met
him only hours ago, Parker let his control slip. His
lips thinned as he continued to clench his teeth. Sara
placed her hand on the side of his face, loving the
feel of that coarse hair beneath her palm.

Who knew she was a beard girl?

Her thumb slid over the puckered scar barely
peeking from the hair on his jawline. Parker circled her wrist with his fingers and eased her hand
aside. His eyes were solely on her now and his body
had relaxed beneath hers. The quiet of the night
surrounded them and reality was like a smack to
the face.

Damn it. This is why she never wanted to do flings

or one-night stands. This is why she wanted a significant other. Because when the sex was over, they could talk or just relax together and not feel the need for words. But considering they didn't know each other, there was only an awkward silence that surrounded them and she had no idea what to do next.

So she started by getting off of his lap and pretending she didn't just have a life-altering experience that would fuel her fantasies forever.

She hadn't been cold on this cozy patio until now, but standing before him naked with every vulnerability exposed, a chill spiraled through her. Sara glanced around for her clothes and saw her underwear sticking out from under the comforter. No need to get hypothermia along with her night of other firsts.

"Regrets already?" he questioned.

Without glancing his way, she plucked one article at a time up off the floor and willed herself not to rush. She had to be casual and calm…two emotions she was certainly not feeling right now.

"I don't do regrets," she stated with her back to him as she tried to remember what had happened to her bra. "But it's time for me to go."

Parker came to his feet. He shifted behind her and Sara stilled. His warmth seemed to reach her before his hand slid to her waist. Her breath caught in her throat as he eased his fingers across her abdomen and his palm flattened against her. With a gentle tug, he pulled her back against his bare chest.

Sara closed her eyes and knew she was losing this battle…whatever this battle was at this point. She'd lost herself this evening…and she wasn't sorry.

"Stay for a while," he whispered, his warm breath washing over her and sending a whole host of post-coital shivers.

"I can't stay all night."

"I didn't ask for all night," he corrected. "We haven't tried the hot tub yet."

Sara laughed and glanced over her shoulder. "You're ready for another round?"

Parker smoothed her hair from her face and circled her waist with his hands. He lifted her until she was flush against him and he carried her toward the hot tub on the other side of the patio.

"I will be," he assured her. "You're not leaving all tense like that. Apparently I didn't do a good job of relaxing you."

Parker eased her hands apart, sending the pile of her clothes back to the floor. After removing the cover, he lifted her over the edge of the hot tub like she weighed nothing at all…which was pretty damn hot. The warmth of the water sent shivers through her. She always loved a nice hot bath, and this was just another level of pleasure.

Sara moved toward one of the built-in seats and eased down. Parker tapped a couple of buttons and jets hit her back. When he climbed in with her, her body started completely over with arousal and desire. How was that even possible? Moments ago she

was ready to leave and take her memories with her…
Looks like she had more memories to make here.

Parker's hands rested on either side of her shoulders as he leaned down to meet her gaze.

"I plan on taking more time with you," he told her. "Unless you really wanted to leave."

He took one hand, disappearing beneath the water. Suddenly his fingertips eased between her legs. Sara gasped and eased further down into the water.

"I think I can stay a bit longer."

A naughty smile crept over his lips. "I thought you might."

Four

"It's a miracle you're still alive."

Delilah was always the dramatic sister, always the careful one who worried. And with Elise out of town with Antonio on their honeymoon, Dee clearly thought she needed to take up the slack of the absent sister.

"It's not a miracle." Sara came to stand behind her desk and smoothed down her cropped blazer. "I had a one-night stand. They happen."

"Not to you," Delilah fired back. "You're the happily-ever-after girl, not the happy-for-now girl."

"Well, maybe I am while I'm waiting for 'the one' to drop into my life." A pang of envy pierced her...and not for the first time. "I texted you my whereabouts and when I was safely back home. So stop acting like my mother."

Delilah jerked back and immediately Sara regretted her words. She blew out a sigh. The three girls had all been in the foster care system as infants, then all adopted by Milly Hawthorne as she tracked down each one. The single woman raised them as her own—it wasn't until her death nearly a year ago that they found out she had actually been their biological aunt and Milly's sister had been their mother. All this time the girls thought they were all adopted sisters and really good friends, but they actually shared a mother.

Their fathers, though, that was another story because they all had different dads. The girls had so many questions, but their mother had passed while in prison serving time for drug possession and now with Milly gone, they were left to their own devices to find their own answers.

"I'm sorry." Sara shifted her hair over her shoulder, her nerves getting the best of her. "I didn't mean that. I know you care, but I assure you that I'm not naive and I'm not careless. I'm a single woman who is just having fun."

Delilah stared for another minute before she offered a wide grin.

"Since you're safe and you didn't get abducted, how much fun did you have exactly? I almost came to your house yesterday, but Cam stopped me. He said you were a grown woman having a bit of fun."

Fun, indeed. The images of Parker and her on the patio sofa and in the hot tub flooded her mind…as if she'd been able to think of anything else since she'd left Saturday night. She'd never gotten his real name, never knew his story or where he was from. But, oh mercy, did she have the memories that would last a lifetime. Her body still tingled.

"I'll take your sly grin and silence as a good indicator of how your night went."

Sara smiled at her sister and shrugged. "I'm less nervous for my interview now that I have something else occupying my thoughts."

"I still cannot believe Ian Ford is doing a piece on Angel's Share." Delilah shook her head and rested her hands on the back of the leather chair across from Sara's desk. "You better hope like hell he doesn't tarnish our reputation."

"He won't."

She hoped.

"Ian is notorious for making or breaking people and businesses," Delilah went on. "We've got too much at stake for him to put a black cloud over our name here."

"There will be no black cloud," Sara stated. "I promise, he will not be able to construe my words in any manner other than bright and shiny."

"Speaking of, what are you wearing to the Christmas at the Castle?"

Their very first holiday gala was right around the corner and as of this moment, Sara had about three dresses she wanted to wear. Of course other days, she hated all the dresses and wanted to start completely over and have someone else tell her what to wear.

"I have no idea. I can't decide if I want to do festive and bright or classy and dark or wintery white. I went ahead and made us all an appointment at Queen so we can shop together once Elise is back."

"Excuse me."

Sara's office door opened and her assistant, Molly, poked her head in. "Mr. Ford is here to see you."

Sara glanced to the time on her computer and realized she and Delilah had been talking for a while and Mr. Ford was a punctual man—though she expected nothing less. No time for nerves or second guesses now.

"Send him on in," Sara replied with a smile.

"I'm not ready for my part of the interview," Delilah whispered, her eyes wide with worry. "I'm not scheduled to talk to him until the end of the week."

Sara shrugged. "Looks like you're going to meet him now."

She came around her desk and smoothed her hair behind her shoulders, making sure her smile remained firmly in place. Despite the nerves in her belly, she needed to put on a strong front and she was actually glad time had gotten away from them, because she wanted Delilah by her side and there was no time for her sister to scurry out now.

Ian Ford was well-known in the journalism industry. But unless you met the man face-to-face, nobody really knew what he looked like. Any social media account he had was all about his work and zero photographs. Supposedly, he never did public appearances. Ian must have to jump through hoops to keep his image protected…but why? He exuded mystery, which was just all part of his allure…or so his publisher likely thought. It mostly just annoyed the hell out of Sara because she'd tried everything to find him online and absolutely nothing came up.

Looked like she was about to see the man behind the facade.

Her office door opened once again and Sara nearly fell back against her desk. Ian Ford was no stranger. She'd seen him before…she'd seen every inch of him, in fact.

When his eyes met hers, there was no emotion. Absolutely nothing from those secretive dark eyes of his.

As if "Parker" hadn't seen every inch of her as well.

Hell. Oh, hell no.

So "Jane" was actually Sara Hawthorne, co-owner of Angel's Share, and the sole reason for his trip up north.

Fan-freakin'-tastic.

As if he didn't have the weight of the proverbial world on his shoulders already, the one time he gives in to temptation and has a one-night stand, he discovers it is with his subject.

Nothing like looking like a total ass of a professional with one foot out the door of his publisher. He said he'd do Nigel one last favor with this piece... but sleeping with the subject sure as hell was not what either of them had in mind. This is precisely why he always chose his own subject matter and he never traveled for business.

"I'm Delilah." The striking woman off to the side stepped forward with her hand extended. "We're so thrilled to have you here. Our sister, Elise, is out of the country right now. Sara is the best one out of all of us, though. You're definitely in good hands."

Ian forced his gaze away from the clearly shocked Sara and shook Delilah's hand. The sisters looked nothing alike. There was definitely a story there, and he planned on finding out every secret and bit of backstory with each of these women... more so with Sara, but those findings wouldn't be going in his article.

"It's a pleasure," he told her, shaking her hand, then stepping back to turn his attention to Sara. "Are we doing a joint interview or sticking with the itinerary?"

Delilah waved her hand in the air. "I'm stepping out. We were talking business and got carried away with time. I am looking forward to our talk later in the week."

Ian nodded. "As am I."

Delilah glanced to her sister. "Sara, I'll get with you later."

Then she walked out of the office, leaving with a soft click of the door.

"Did you know who I was?" Sara growled the second they were alone.

Her dark eyes narrowed into slits, showing him a totally different side than the Sara—or Jane—that he knew.

"Of course not. You told me your name was Jane."

"Jane is my middle name."

Ian laughed. "Parker is my middle name."

Sara started to smile, but quickly recovered, narrowing her eyes again. "You want me to believe you didn't go online to see the sisters who own Angel's Share?"

"Of course I did, but the picture on the site is the three of you in front of the castle and the span is large. And your individual bios all have the Angel's Share logo instead of a photo. So, no. I had no idea you were the person I was interviewing when we met the other night."

She continued to glare and shoot invisible daggers like *he* had done something wrong here. She sure as hell didn't think he was doing anything wrong the other night…she'd even begged for more.

Filled with a new level of frustration and annoyance, Ian shrugged. "Believe what you want. This assignment came to me when I thought I was done with *Elite*, but I'm doing this as a favor to my editor. Then I'm done. I'll do a kick-ass job, but I don't need to scroll through your social media trying to uncover who each of the sisters are. I believe in getting that knowledge firsthand."

"You got that on Saturday night."

"Sara, I didn't know who you were," Ian said, trying to keep his frustration in check.

"Well, I tried to find pictures of you," she retorted, crossing her arms over her chest.

Ian willed himself to keep his gaze locked onto hers and not check out how perfectly deliciously that bright blue suit hugged her curves. He could still feel those curves beneath his hands, could still feel her delicate touch and hear her soft moans from the passion they shared.

Damn it. He needed to get a grip. Maybe he could find a way to wrap up this interview a little early so he wasn't subjected to temptation any longer than necessary.

"Why are there no photos anywhere?"

Her question pulled him back to the moment and the fact that she might be sexy, but she was still seething.

"I've never seen someone who literally cannot be found anywhere online," she added in disbelief.

Yeah, and he paid an exorbitant amount to keep his anonymity. There was no way in hell he was going to get into all the reasons why. He'd never let anyone in on his personal life and all of his issues, so there was certainly no chance of him exposing his vulnerabilities with his one-night stand.

"Are we doing the interview in here?" he asked, forcing her hand into professionalism. "Or are you showing me around the distillery?"

Sara stared him down for another moment before dropping her arms and blowing out a sigh. That anger clearly transitioning to frustration.

"Listen, we need to discuss the other night before we just dive headfirst into work."

Ian rested his hands on his hips and really wished he'd done that research on each of the women of Angel's Share. Since this was to be his last piece for *Elite*, he didn't necessarily believe he needed to hone in on each remarkable woman.

He hadn't recognized Sara at the Quiet Distil because she was out of her element and he'd never seen a close-up picture of her, so there was nothing he could do at this point. He couldn't turn back time or have a redo of Saturday night.

He also couldn't have regrets about that night... he *wouldn't*. Everything about their heated affair had been magical and perfect. And each and every moment would have stayed locked in his memory bank had he not walked into "Jane's" office this morning.

"Nothing to discuss," he corrected. "We hadn't planned on seeing each other again, so now we just pretend it didn't happen and focus on work, which is the only reason I'm here."

Oh, those dark eyes seemed to grow even blacker. Maybe she could get sexier, because even anger looked damn good on her.

"Forget it happened?" she fired back. "Do you just have some magical switch you turn off and on?"

He wished. If he was actually as stony as people thought, maybe he wouldn't feel so damn much. He'd done a hell of a job compartmentalizing his emotions over the years and he didn't intend to stop now—that's the only way he made it day by day. Despite the passionate evening they'd shared two days ago, that didn't mean they should or would have a replay.

"I'm leaving that night right where it belongs," he informed her. "In the past, where we *both* agreed it would stay."

She pursed her lips and his body betrayed him. Despite his words, he'd thought of little else since she left his place and seeing those red lips puckered only reminded him of just how damn much he'd enjoyed that mouth.

Getting aroused during the job had never been an issue before…then again, he'd never taken a stranger back to his place for a one-night stand, either. Relationships of any kind had never appealed to him. He refused to put his heart on the line for anything or anyone ever again…no matter how temporary. Work was all that he could control, all that really mattered at the end of the day.

"You're completely different from the man I met at the Quiet Distil."

"Same man," he assured her. "Today is just a different aspect of my life."

When she continued to stare as if trying to figure him out, Ian pulled in a deep breath. There was no way he'd let anyone try to get inside his world, so she might as well not even try. Yes, they had an amazing night that shouldn't still be in his every waking thought, but that was his problem. He was only here as a courtesy and commitment to his editor, nothing more.

"Just like that, huh?" she murmured.

Ian shrugged. "There's no other way to move on, and we both agreed at the time that night was a one-time thing. So, are we doing the interview in here or would you like to show me around first?"

He waited on more backlash, but Sara squared her shoulders and tipped that defiant chin. Damn, she shouldn't be sexier when she was angry, but she was. Again, his problem and something he would deal with on his own. Once he could shift her into that subject zone and see her only as his job, he'd be just fine. Right?

"I need some fresh air." She circled her desk and crossed her office, then grabbed her coat off a peg near the door. "We'll walk the grounds and I'll give you the history of Angel's Share."

He had a feeling the brisk air was the least of his worries, because the iciness from Sara Hawthorne already had him feeling frigid.

Five

"And that brings us back to the main entrance of the castle."

Sara had given every detail and fact she'd ever learned or discovered about Angel's Share from the time it was built all the way up until now. She was nearly frozen, but she deserved to be punished after her poor professional skills in thinking Ian might carry over any feelings he had from the other night.

She wasn't naive, but this entire situation made her feel like a teenager getting dumped for the first time. Totally blindsided from a situation she'd invested too many thoughts into.

Maybe if she hadn't been caught so off guard, she wouldn't have nearly passed out when he stepped into her office. Thankfully Delilah hadn't noticed anything off, or if she did, she was saving that conversation for later.

As they crossed the stone path and the iconic drawbridge leading to the front entrance, Ian reached out and opened the door for her. He gestured her in ahead of him and she gladly stepped inside to get out of the winter elements. At least he still had manners, even if he was still pretending that they hadn't thoroughly enjoyed pleasuring each other only two short days ago.

The warmth from the castle enveloped her as soon as she stepped over that threshold. The old stone fireplace off to the right wasn't just for aesthetics and an amazing backdrop for photo shoots. The heat instantly made guests feel cozy during the cold months in Kentucky. Plus with the beauty of the fresh greenery draped over anything that was stationary, the wintery ambiance had an even cozier vibe.

Several workers moved about from one direction to another, a few stopped to chat, while others seemed to be on a mission. Sara was so proud of all they'd accomplished, not just for her and her sisters, but the fact that they employed over one hundred local folks. This truly was like one big happy family.

"Is there usually this much activity during the day?" Ian asked as he came to stand next to her.

"Not typically, but with the Christmas at the Castle gala in just two weeks, we're a little busier than

usual. More decor, definitely more trees and gar-
lands and lights. Mistletoe, too. Can't have a Christmas party without it."

"Is this gala something you do every year?"

"This will be our first, but one we hope to make
an annual tradition."

Ian glanced back down to his notepad and jotted
more notes. He'd barely looked at her since leaving her office earlier. He certainly hadn't touched
her or made any personal references. No personal
questions, either.

This whole charade was really getting old. It was
impossible for her to just fake all of this nonsense.
Yes, they were both professionals in their fields and,
yes, Ian Ford was a celebrity journalist, but at the
end of the day, they were both real people. Well,
she was. She was starting to wonder if he was hard-
hearted or simply robotic. This was definitely not
the man she'd been with the other night. This Ian
Ford was exactly like she'd imagined: cold, stoic,
all business…boring.

The man from Saturday night was the complete
opposite. Sexy, intriguing, attentive, passionate.
There had been nothing icy about "Parker."

Then again, they'd both been someone else that
night. She'd faked being bold and assertive and now
she was her true self. Perhaps he'd done the same.
Maybe this stony man before her was the real Ian.
Shame that, because she wouldn't mind meeting
"Parker" again. Parker made her want to be that

bold woman, that woman who wasn't afraid to go after what she wanted.

"You're staring."

His statement forced her attention back to him and she blinked to return to the moment. He hadn't even looked up from his notes and he'd known she was staring. Lovely. Could she be any less professional?

"I'm not staring," she corrected, though she totally had been. "I'm waiting on you to finish up before we move on."

His lips thinned as he continued writing and Sara blinked as she glanced away. The last thing she needed to be looking at was his lips. She needed to focus on this interview because despite what had already transpired between them, Ian was going to write a piece on Angel's Share and with the launch of their ten-year bourbon just months ago and their rise to fame and success, she couldn't afford to have a black cloud hovering over them.

Elise, Delilah, and Sara all invested so much into this business—Milly, too. Their adoptive mother had cheered them every step of the way and, unfortunately, had passed just short of the ten-year bourbon rollout. But Sara knew she was smiling down on them and proud of what her girls had accomplished.

Sara just wished Milly would have disclosed the truth while she'd been alive. Why not just come out and say that she's their biological aunt? That her sister was their mother and the woman had a drug problem? Not telling them might have protected them for so long, but ultimately the pain still entered in once they discovered the truth.

"You still with me?"

Sara shifted her focus back to Ian, who stared at her with his brows drawn together. Great, now she'd zoned out on him. He probably thought she wanted to be anywhere but in this moment…which was partly true.

With a deep breath, Sara pulled herself together and eased out of her coat.

"Are you ready to head back to my office and start the interview? Or would you like to break for lunch?"

"Where is a good place around here to grab something?" he asked.

She folded her coat over her arm and started walking toward her office on the second floor. He fell in step beside her and part of her wanted to tell him a few places to go, to give herself a break from his presence, but that damn voice in her head kept nagging at her. Anybody else, whom she hadn't slept with, she would offer for them to stay and she'd have something brought in. She should treat him no differently.

"I actually have a favorite and one call will have anything you want delivered." They reached the landing and started to turn, but she stopped and looked up at him. "I figure being from the south, you don't want to go out in the cold any more than you have to, and I just had you in and out for the past two hours."

The muscle in his jaw clenched. "I'm actually from Ohio, but I've lived in Florida for years. I don't like the cold."

Why was he so intense? Something in her innocent question pushed a trigger within him and she shouldn't want to know more…but she did. She had a feeling trying to figure this man out would be about as easy as cuddling up with a porcupine.

"Let's get to my office and we'll order in," she suggested. "We can have a working lunch…unless you want to ask personal questions."

"I don't."

Of course not. Well, she couldn't compartmentalize as easily as he could, so he'd just have to live with it. She wasn't going to walk on eggshells or be someone else just because he was uncomfortable.

They reached her office door and she punched in the code, then gestured him in ahead of her. Once inside, she closed the door and turned to face him.

There it was. That crackling tension she'd felt at the Quiet Distil. He had that damn stare that made her wonder if he could see into her soul. He hadn't moved far into the room, actually stood only a few feet away from her. He'd said he didn't want to discuss that night, but his eyes said he wouldn't mind an encore performance.

Sara pulled in a deep breath and turned to hang her coat on the peg by her door.

"Let me have your coat," she told him, looping her tag over the hanger.

When she shifted back around, Ian had removed his coat, and her breath caught in her throat. He had on another one of those vests with his dress shirt and dress pants—dove gray this time. Why did he have to look like he just walked off a movie set from the 1930s? And why did the man's wardrobe turn her on so much?

Ian handed over the garment and Sara reached out, her hand immediately grabbing his instead of the coat. Her eyes darted up to his and she wasn't surprised to find him staring right back.

Without a word, she snagged the coat and hung it next to hers. Sara needed to gather her words before she addressed all of this tension because she couldn't handle the rest of the week the way this morning had gone. Being close, talking business, pretending like they hadn't shared flirty banter and a heated night.

"You told me you did weddings."

Sara jerked back at his statement before she'd ever even had a chance to say anything.

"That's not what I said at all," she countered. "I said I helped with weddings, which I had just done for my sister and we are currently working on one for the governor's daughter in the spring. And don't get so high and mighty when you didn't give me your real name. If we'd done that off the bat, none of this would have happened."

Something even darker came over his eyes as he closed the distance between them. Sara's breath caught in her throat and she had to force herself not to move, not to reach out to see if that icy exterior melted beneath her touch. She waited.

"None of this would have happened," he murmured, his eyes dropping to her mouth. "Do you have regrets?"

"No."

How could she have any shame or guilt over one of the most thrilling nights of her life? All she regretted was how this reunion was playing out.

"We need to discuss what happened so we can move on," she insisted.

Ian's lips thinned. "What do you want to talk about so badly? Does that night replay over and over in your head? Are you wondering how we can work together on this article and not rip at each other's clothes? Are you wondering if I'll make a move?"

Well…yes, actually. Yes to all of those questions, but the way he worded them made her sound desperate and she might be achy and needy, but she definitely wasn't desperate.

And she wasn't the only one having a difficult time. She might not know him well, but she wasn't blind. The way he'd stared at her, the way he'd been so attentive the other night, there was no way he could turn off those feelings. She refused to believe it.

Maybe when he'd first arrived this morning she'd

thought him stony, but he'd stepped into her office moments ago and looked at her as if ripping her clothes off was precisely what he'd been wanting to do.

"Is that what *you* want?" she asked. "To make a move?"

The muscle in his jaw clenched, drawing her attention to that puckered scar. His beard covered a good bit of the old injury, but the jagged edge peeked out above the dark hair. She'd also felt the uneven skin beneath her touch the other night.

Unable to resist, Sara reached up and trailed her fingertip along his jaw.

"You're a mysterious man," she whispered. "With a past I can't help but wonder about."

That flash of desire quickly vanished as Ian took a step back, then another, then ultimately turned to head across her office. Was he trying to purposely keep this wall of division between them? Because he seemed like he was having a hell of a time battling his self-control.

"Keep wondering," he commanded with his back to her as he stared out the arched window.

Sara clenched her hand at her side, trying to hold tight to that warmth from his body. She shouldn't want more. She should ignore her urges and move on. Ian clearly waged a war between his own wants and he seemed to have no problem pushing her aside.

That shouldn't cause a piercing pain, but...

Sara smoothed her hair away from her face and

took a deep breath before heading toward her desk. She was supposed to be ordering them a lunch, not rehashing Saturday night or even hoping for something more. Ian wasn't a "something more" type of guy, he'd made that much very clear.

Obviously two people could be physically compatible, but that's where it ended. She wasn't naive, she knew what the other night was and wasn't. She'd just been caught so off guard and there was so much more she wanted to know about Ian. She had so many questions, but from the look of his rigid shoulders and the silence that had settled heavy between them, Sara would have to keep wondering…just like he'd suggested.

Six

"Well, how did it go?"

Sara glanced up from her phone to her sister standing in the doorway.

Settling back into her desk chair, Sara shrugged. "It went."

"That doesn't sound promising." Delilah stepped into Sara's office and closed the door at her back. "Was he a jerk? Did he ask difficult questions? Do you think he's planning to ruin us with the article?"

"No, no and no."

Delilah came to a stop as her brows drew in. "Then what was the problem?"

Sara didn't know if she should reveal the full truth now, or tell her later when Elise came back, or if she should just keep everything a secret. But there had already been so many secrets in their lives that Sara didn't want to add to them.

If Sara had learned anything over the past year, it was that family was more important than ever. She desperately needed someone's advice before she had a total meltdown. There were too many raw, fresh emotions swirling around inside her and she trusted two people with her life…and one was on her honeymoon. That left Delilah.

"I slept with Ian."

Dee's face completely morphed into shock, confusion and anger all at once. Her eyes widened, those sculpted brows shot up and her mouth dropped. She remained still, too still, as she continued to stare.

"What the hell, Sara? You just met the man this morning."

Sara chewed the inside of her cheek for a moment. "We met before."

Delilah blinked, then gasped. "No. Please tell me he's not the man from the other night."

"Okay. I won't tell you that."

Dee closed her eyes and blew out a frustrated sigh. Maybe Sara shouldn't have said anything, but she was hoping once the initial shock wore off, her sister could offer some sound advice.

Granted, Sara was still in shock herself, so she shouldn't be expecting a miracle here.

"You've got to be kidding me," Dee muttered as

she crossed the office and sank into the leather club chair across from Sara's desk. "Of all the people in the world you choose for a one-night stand, you chose Ian freakin' Ford?"

"It's not like I knew who he was," Sara defended. "You know the man is so elusive. It never crossed my mind he was the stranger I flirted with at the bourbon bar."

Delilah pinched the bridge of her nose and the lighting caught the emerald-cut diamond on her ring finger. As if Sara needed that visual reminder of just how Delilah's life was on the path Sara wanted to be on.

"Okay, we need to fix this," Dee stated, dropping her hands into her lap.

"And how do we do that?" Sara asked. "I can't un-sex him."

"Now is not the time for jokes," Delilah scolded.

"That wasn't a joke. I literally have no idea what to do."

"Well, did you guys at least address the issue?"

A vivid image of him hovering over her, looking like he wanted to kiss her, flashed through her mind. But she'd ruined anything Ian had been about to say or do when she reached up and touched his scar. What was the story there? Was the scar the sole reason for the beard? Another way for him to hide? Or was that what started his need for anonymity?

So many questions that she couldn't have answered, but that didn't stop her from wondering.

She couldn't get Ian out of her mind for a variety of reasons…mainly her Saturday night experience that still had her tingling.

"Sara. Snap out of it."

Sara blinked and leaned forward, resting her elbows on top of her desk.

"No, we didn't discuss it because he didn't want to." The man had closed up for the rest of the day and they only discussed business. "I brought up that night a couple of times and he only wanted to move forward."

"That's typically how a one-night stand works."

Sara rolled her eyes. "I'm aware. I mean, I'd never had one before, but I assumed. Still, these are unique circumstances and I thought we should clear the air or something. Anything would be better than just ignoring it."

Delilah didn't reply. Silence hovered between them and Sara waited on her sister to give some solid, sound advice that would make all of this awkward tension between Ian and Sara go away. They had several days left together to go through the entire bourbon process, not to mention the other spirits Angel's Share sold. They were going over every aspect of the company from conception up until now. Ian wanted all the answers, and that could only boil down to hours of alone time.

Which was the last thing she needed with a man who made her toes curl when he simply sent a stare her way.

Why this guy? Why did she have to get so wrapped up with the one person who should be off-limits? Had she met him in a professional setting first, Sara would have just thought he was some arrogant jerk. Sexy and intriguing in that dark, stealthy way, but a jerk nonetheless.

"So now what?" Dee asked after a moment.

"That's sort of what I was hoping you'd tell me," Sara replied. "I mean, clearly we have a kick-ass company and we're growing each day. I'm not at all worried about the professional side of this situation."

"Maybe you should just take his lead and move on," Dee suggested.

Sara mulled that thought over in her mind and finally nodded. "You're right. Trying to get him to talk or rehash it all would only make me look desperate."

"Please don't tell me you want to sleep with him again? That was a one and done, right?"

Sara laughed. "Of course. Now that I know who he is, I definitely can't sleep with him again."

"If he wasn't Ian Ford, you'd be right after him."

Sara shrugged. "If circumstances were different, you bet I would. Parker was a totally different man than Ian."

Delilah's brows lifted. "Parker?"

"The name he gave me at the Quiet Distil. I was Jane and he was Parker. We both used our middle names."

Delilah closed her eyes and shook her head. "One-night stand and role-playing. Lovely."

Sara couldn't help but laugh. "We weren't role-playing. We just didn't want to go into personal details since we hadn't planned on seeing each other again. Granted, we didn't plan on sleeping together, either. We were just flirting and talking, then the bar closed, and then there was a hot tub."

Delilah held up her hands. "No details necessary. I get it."

Sara's cell vibrated on her desk and she glanced to see Ian's name pop up. Her eyes darted to Delilah, who had also redirected her attention toward the cell.

"Well, well, well," Delilah crooned. "Perhaps he wants to chat after all."

Sara didn't want to snatch up the phone like some teen who needed the attention from a popular boy. She'd never chased after a man in her life and she sure as hell didn't intend to start now. Oh, she might have been a little assertive with Ian the other night, but that was merely going after what she wanted.

Determined, that's what Milly always called her. A pang of nostalgia hit her at the thought of the only mother she'd ever known. This would be one of those circumstances where she could use some motherly advice.

"Aren't you going to see what he wants?"

Sara glanced from her sister to the phone. She eased into her seat and turned slightly back and forth, weighing her decision and how she wanted to proceed with this web she had spun around herself.

"I will. He's not going anywhere."

Delilah sighed and pushed to her feet, instantly reaching for the cell. "Well, I want to know what he says."

Dee snatched the device before Sara could and all Sara could do at this point was hold her breath. She watched Delilah's face for any sign of what Ian had sent, but all Dee did was chew on her bottom lip.

"Well? What is it?"

"You acted like you didn't care," Delilah reminded her. "Now you want to know?"

Sara stood and rounded her desk, grabbing the cell from her sister. She read the message herself.

I will be in at 1:00 tomorrow

That's it? That's all he wanted to tell her? Wait a second! They'd set their start time for 9:00 a.m. He was now pushing it back several hours.

Okay, fine. Whatever. So he was a professional and not texting her for a booty call. Shouldn't she be glad he didn't think of her that way?

Probably. But she wouldn't mind if he did. Just one more time.

"Sorry, sis." Delilah rested her hand on Sara's arm. "That man has a workaholic reputation for a reason. He's all business, all the time."

"Not all the time," Sara muttered.

Clearly he was in the zone and nothing would pull Ian Ford from this work bubble he'd encased himself in…not even the opportunity for another passionate night.

His loss.

Seven

The online meeting with Nigel had run over and Ian was even later than he had planned getting back to Angel's Share. He figured Sara was still upset with him over...well, everything, so what was one more thing?

This entire interview and article had been a mistake from the second he'd said yes, but Nigel was impossible to say no to. The man had given Ian his crack into journalism when Ian first moved to Miami. Nigel was so much more than a boss or a mentor; he was probably Ian's closest friend. His only friend, really.

Ian had no plans on leaving Miami once he was finished at *Elite* and he had no plans on ending his relationship with Nigel. Ian had become restless with his work lately, always trying to find something more, but nothing was filling that void. Nigel understood and was actually the one to recommend Ian write a book.

Being able to write while working remotely and alone was the only way he wanted to live. He'd gotten comfortable with his lifestyle and just because he needed a fresh restart in his career didn't mean he was ready to change his habits.

Yet he'd gone completely against everything he stood for when he'd picked up Sara in that damn bourbon bar. And maybe the circumstances wouldn't be so bad if she wasn't his subject and if he still didn't want the hell out of her. Seeing her in her element yesterday had only added to her appeal. She'd been so professional and business-oriented. She loved her job and her passion for everything she'd built had come to light.

Having seen her passionate side in business and her pleasure in private had him wondering how often she revealed both sides to the same man.

Ian stepped inside the main entrance of Angel's Share and instantly found himself feeling at home. How ridiculous was that? He'd only been to this distillery once and already he thought he belonged?

Perhaps those unwanted, unexpected emotions stemmed from all the Christmas decor with the fresh evergreens and all the twinkling lights that reminded him of how his mother would decorate.

Or maybe there was something about Sara herself that had touched on a warmth inside him he hadn't known existed.

No matter what, Ian knew for certain he wouldn't be staying here long, so he might as well just shove these emotions out of his head and his heart. He was here for a job, not to get all nostalgic. The memories he'd suppressed needed to stay buried because nothing would mess him up more than reliving that nightmare all over again.

"Mr. Ford?"

Ian turned to Delilah, who was crossing the lobby. She had a wide smile on her face, her dark hair smoothed over one shoulder, and a red pantsuit. There was something to be said for having three strong, powerful women running a successful business. They'd set themselves up for a unique success that was unmatched in the industry.

"It's so great to see you again." She greeted him with a firm handshake. "Sara is handling a minor hiccup at the moment, so I will be taking you to our VIP room for an exclusive tasting. You will get all the perks of one of our elite clients so you can see exactly how we conduct our business."

"That sounds interesting. I'm definitely up for a tasting. I actually tried one of your batches at the Quiet Distil the other evening."

Delilah started walking and Ian fell into step beside her as they made their way toward the staircase. As they started to climb to the second story,

Ian wondered if Sara actually had an emergency or if she was avoiding him. He'd be lying if he didn't admit he was a little disappointed. He'd wanted his experience to be overseen by Sara. He wanted to see her as much as he could while he was here. Perhaps that made him a glutton, but he couldn't just ignore the fact that he found her way too damn intriguing.

Delilah led Ian down a corridor and up another flight of steps until they reached a room surrounded with stone walls. This part of the castle definitely had to be an original portion, but they'd modernized the area with glass shelving that housed their various bottles of bourbon and their specialty gin. They also displayed their tumbler sets with the Angel's Share logo etched into the glasses.

Everything about this distillery exuded class and money. Was it any wonder the nation, hell, the world, had fallen in love with these three women? He'd spent the morning on the phone with other distillers to get their take on Angel's Share. No deep dark secrets revealed, just a good dose of healthy envy over Angel's Share's accomplishments.

Delilah gestured for him to take a seat in the leather chair opposite where she stood. The raw-edged table between them had a nice, neat row of testers lined up. Ian unbuttoned his coat and slid it off.

"I'll take that for you," Delilah offered. "My apologies. I should have grabbed that first thing."

"No problem at all."

Something clearly occupied her mind and he

wondered if that same something was what kept Sara from coming in here now. He wondered if the problem was business or personal, but had to quickly remind himself that neither circumstance was his concern.

Delilah skirted the table and took his coat, then hung it on a small hook near the door where they came in. Ian waited until she was back before he took a seat in the club chair.

"We'll start from your left and move our way down to the right," she started. "This first one is our ten-year that we unveiled just a few months ago."

"I believe that is the one I had the other evening." Ian reached for the glass and swirled the contents. "The aroma is amazing."

He took one sip, letting the flavors come to life against his taste buds, then he took another.

"Yes," he confirmed. "I had this at the Quiet Distil."

"Where you met Sara."

Ian's eyes darted up to Delilah's and she merely held his gaze without a smile, without any emotion whatsoever.

Okay, that was certainly a plot twist he hadn't expected in his day. Obviously Sara had said something to her sister, but Ian didn't know what all she had told her, so he'd be best to keep things light here.

"We did meet there," he agreed. "We had no clue who the other person was, but we had some great conversations."

Delilah pursed her lips as she quirked a brow.

Oh, yeah. She knew the whole story. Damn it.

How could he keep up his image, his reputation, his *professionalism* if he was going around having sex with the subject before they even got started?

Ian sat the shot glass back down and weighed his next words carefully.

"I have to assume by that disapproving frown, you are fully aware of what happened."

"I'm aware." Delilah flattened her palms onto the table as she leaned in slightly. "I'm not getting into any of that, but what I do want to address is our business. I'm hoping you're professional enough to keep that personal interaction out of your article."

Ian scoffed. "You think I'd mention what happened?"

Delilah shook her head. "No, but I don't want that to hinder your view of Angel's Share or any of us."

Delilah had to be the peacemaker and she clearly seemed worried about what all he'd put into his project. Did she think that he would be harsh simply because Sara picked him up in a bar?

Okay, maybe he picked her up, but whatever.

"I'm professional enough," he assured her. "Just like I assume you didn't tamper with these drinks now that you know I slept with your sister."

Delilah stared for a moment before she laughed and pulled over a stool. "Now that it's settled we are both professionals, let's keep this sampling on track."

"That's it?" he asked. "You're not going to warn me about hurting your sister or say something about how amazing she is?"

Delilah crossed her legs and placed her hands on her lap. "We both know Sara is one of a kind in the very best of ways. She's giving, comforting, always seeing the bright side of things…everything that embodies the perfect human. I'm more jaded with life, but Sara can also be a little naive at times. She truly sees the good in everyone, but I won't warn you. She's a grown woman and while she may have stars in her eyes and be looking for that happily-ever-after, she would never forgive me if she thought I was even having this conversation with you."

"Then why are you?" he asked, reaching for the next glass.

Delilah shrugged. "Because I care about Sara and Angel's Share. Family is everything to us and even though she can certainly take care of herself, that doesn't mean I can't play the protective older sister at times."

Ian sipped on the bourbon and welcomed the warmth and smoky flavor.

"Sara's lucky to have you," he finally told her.

"We're lucky to have each other," Delilah corrected. "Do you have siblings?"

His personal life was sure as hell not the area he wanted to delve into.

"I'm an only child." He sat the glass back down. "Which bourbon was that?"

"That is the special recipe we came up with for one of the pubs in Spain." Delilah pointed to the next one. "This was also created for Rodriguez's. Those restaurants are owned by Elise's husband."

"The sister that just got married?"

Delilah nodded. "Yes. His family has a string of upscale pubs and restaurants in Spain. That's actually how he and my sister met. He came here to look into bourbons."

"And found more than he was looking for."

"I'm sorry I'm late."

Ian turned toward the door and was glad he was sitting down. Sara came striding in wearing a body-hugging green pencil dress and nude heels, which only made her shapely legs look even sexier. With her hair flowing around her shoulders and that red lipstick, Ian wondered if he should just stick with Delilah for the day to avoid further temptation.

"Are you doing a tasting or filling him in on the family secrets?" Sara asked as she came to stand beside her sister.

"A little of both."

Delilah and Sara shot each other a look that had to be some sibling, silent-speaking communication thing. He'd never had that and didn't understand a bond so deep. But he understood love and family, and these two had something special.

"I can finish if you have something else to do," Delilah offered.

Sara glanced to Ian and his gut tightened with that instant arousal…just like the other night when they'd first met.

"I've got this."

Sara continued to hold his gaze as she replied to her sister.

"Are you sure, Sara—"

"We're fine, and that issue I had will have to be discussed later."

Ian watched as the women exchanged another look and the journalist in him wanted to know the details and what had been so important. He'd originally thought Sara was trying to dodge him or any interaction, but after seeing the smoldering look she'd given him, he had to believe something had happened behind the scenes.

Delilah nodded and focused back on Ian. "I look forward to my interview so we can continue our discussion."

Ian couldn't help but stifle a laugh because that almost sounded like a threat…or a promise, he really couldn't tell. Regardless, he gave a nod because he never backed down from a challenge. He had a feeling each of these women would challenge him in a variety of ways.

The click of Delilah's heels echoed in the spacious room as she let herself out. The moment the door closed, Ian met Sara's intense stare.

"What held you up?"

He shouldn't have asked—he actually wasn't going to, but the question just slipped out. He wasn't sorry, though. He did want to know what was going on even if none of this was his concern. That's how he'd gotten such a stellar reputation. He asked the questions people didn't want to answer and somehow got them talking.

"I had a personal matter that needed my immediate attention."

She crossed her arms over her chest and glanced down to the shot glasses. "Looks like you have a few more to go."

"In a minute," he told her. "Something kept you from our appointment and you still seem a little flustered."

"Our appointment?" she questioned with the quirk of one arched dark brow. "Would that be the appointment you changed on me last night?"

"I had a last-minute meeting with my boss at noon that couldn't be moved."

"My appointment couldn't be moved either."

Sara squared her shoulders and didn't blink, as if silently daring him to keep on this topic. He wasn't a stupid man, but he was determined and tenacious. Maybe he wouldn't dig into her personal life right this second, but he would get there and she likely wouldn't even know he'd done so. He wasn't the top journalist in the field for nothing.

"I was just learning about the batches of Angel's Share that are going to Spain."

Sara blinked, clearly taken off guard at his change of the subject. Or perhaps she was surprised he gave in.

"Yes, my brother-in-law was thrilled to have several options to offer his customers. I heard Dee telling you about him."

"So he and Elise fell in love over tastings?" he asked, reaching for another glass.

Sara let out a soft laugh that shouldn't send warmth spreading through him…but that sweet sound was impossible to dismiss.

"I believe they fell in love when they were locked in our cellar during a thunderstorm and power outage."

Ian eased forward a little more and held on to the glass, but was much more interested in hearing this story. "I'm not sure one night together can constitute as love."

"For them it did," she countered, her stare never wavering.

Maybe he should have kept on the topic of her personal life instead of dancing around the topic of a one-night stand. Or love. That sure as hell was one area he didn't want to get into.

Ian sipped the next sample, needing time to figure out exactly how to approach Sara and the work he should be doing here. He'd never been in a position like this before and it was damn uncomfortable wanting a woman and knowing she was off-limits.

He should have made her off-limits from the start, but he'd been in a vulnerable spot that night and in she walked—wearing the same troubled look he'd seen in the mirror. He'd thought they could just keep each other company over a few drinks. He should have known that would be a mistake, considering that was so far out of his comfort zone.

Why Sara? Why couldn't he have met anyone else from Benton Springs and shared a passionate night? Then he wouldn't be so tied up in knots and struggling to keep his professional persona in place.

"Why don't you ever let anyone see the man behind the words?"

Sara's question hit him like a punch to the gut. Nobody was ever so bold with him and she continued to stare like she wasn't about to back down. Well, too damn bad.

"If your personal life is off-limits, so is mine."

Her brow quirked and Sara merely nodded in understanding. The silence settled between them, heavy and thick like the tension that had encompassed them from the moment he realized who she actually was.

Sara blew out a sigh and closed her eyes for the briefest of moments before leveling his gaze once again.

"Perhaps I should have Delilah finish the tastings," she suggested. "This is getting more difficult."

Ian listened to her words, but there was something she wasn't saying. Reading body language was second nature to him in his line of work. He'd always had to read between the lines and take hints from how people responded, or didn't respond, to him.

Sara had a look in her eyes he hadn't seen before. And while he hadn't known her long, he had a feeling the woman he met that first night was the true Sara. That woman had been bold, vibrant, persistent. And while this Sara was all of those things, today there was a look in her eyes he hadn't noticed. Something haunted her or kept that light from shining like before.

And he wasn't about to let her just gloss it over or pretend. She didn't have to be all business right now because clearly an underlying element had rattled her world.

"Let's get out of here," he stated.

Sara blinked and jerked back. "Excuse me?"

Yeah, he had no idea where he was going with this, either, he just knew these walls were closing in on him and she looked like she needed a break. He would be here for a while still, so taking a few hours away from work for both of them might be just what they needed to get back on track.

Ian came to his feet and gestured toward the door. "Let's go."

He didn't wait on her to reply as he headed to snatch his coat from the hanger and head out. Now he just had to figure out what the hell his plans were.

Eight

Sara had no idea how she ended up in the front seat of Ian's rental SUV, but here they were maneuvering through the snow-lined streets of Benton Springs. They'd barely said two words since leaving the distillery and when Delilah had given her a questioning look as they'd been walking out, Sara had merely shrugged.

"Is there a point to this trip?" she finally asked.

He shot her a brief look. "To maintain our sanity."

"Is that a problem for you? Because I'm perfectly fine."

Ian snorted, but said nothing. Maybe he noticed she wasn't fine, but she had to at least put up a good front. No matter what had transpired between them, they were still in a working relationship. And as much as she hated to admit it, she was at his mercy. She was the business owner who had the obligation to cater to her client. This man was an award-winning journalist and she wanted nothing but glowing words in regard to Angel's Share.

The snow started coming down a little harder and she noted Ian slowed; his grip on the wheel had gotten tighter if his white knuckles were any indicator.

"Do you need to pull over and let me drive?" she offered. "I'm used to this unpredictable weather. Warm one day, freak snowstorm the next."

He didn't take his eyes off the road or speak, he merely shook his head. Obviously he wanted to concentrate and needed silence. Whatever. A skiff of snow was no big deal to her, but for someone from Miami, it could be concerning.

When Ian pulled into the lot of her favorite coffee shop, Sara unfastened her seat belt.

"We had coffee right in my office," she informed him.

"We also needed to get out of that atmosphere," he retorted.

Ian opened his door and an immediate blast of cold air filled the interior. He muttered a curse and something about freezing his ass off before the door closed behind him. Like a gentleman, he rounded the hood and opened her door, then extended his hand to help her down.

"Careful," he warned. "There's a little patch of ice here."

Before she could even take a step, Ian wrapped his arm around her waist and lifted her from the ground. He carried her at his side and carefully set her down on the sidewalk.

Why did her heart have to flutter at this gesture? He was merely making sure she didn't embarrass herself by falling, he wasn't playing some chivalrous modern-day knight. He was much too brooding to play the good guy in any situation.

"You been here before?" he asked, nodding toward Rise and Grind.

"All the time. One of my friends from high school opened this place about ten years ago."

Ian shook his head. "I should've known you'd be friends with the owner. Is there a business around this town that you aren't in close contact with the owner?"

Sara thought for a moment, then shook her head. "Not really. We're actually a small town and very supportive of one another."

Snow started to fall once again, dotting Ian's dark hair. The striking contrast captivated her attention and she watched as each flake melted.

"You're staring."

Sara blinked and smiled. "I don't think you mind, do you? I'm freezing. Let's get inside."

He reached for her hand and she knew without a doubt it was to assist her over the snow piles, but part of her loved that strength and warmth from his touch. She shouldn't, *couldn't,* find this man so enchanting. He was not the fairy-tale ending she was looking for. He was a one-night stand and a temporary fling. Nothing more.

And one of these times she'd believe those lies she kept telling herself.

Ian reached for the door and ushered her inside. The cozy atmosphere always boosted her mood. The fresh aroma of coffee, the fire in the old stone fireplace, the dark rich wood floors and the leather chairs could be seen as masculine, but Sara always found Rise and Grind to be a place of strength. Maybe that came from the caffeine, but the decor really spoke to her as something classy, timeless.

Much like the man beside her. She'd never seen him in anything other than a vest, matching dress pants and a white button-up shirt. That was so damn classy and sexy, she was having a difficult time remembering why they shouldn't keep exploring what they'd started the other night.

"Are we staying or getting drinks to go?" she asked.

Ian glanced out the window as snow continued to swirl around. "I didn't realize the weather was going to get this bad."

Sara watched the flurries and shrugged. "You've been in the south too long. This is nothing. Let's grab a seat. They have the absolute best bacon ched-dar scones."

As she headed to the counter, Sara noted they weren't all that busy. Hopefully her favorite spot in the back was available. The barista took her order and Sara turned to see Ian still staring out the win-dow.

"Ian?"

He jerked his attention back to her and crossed the open space. After a moment, he ordered and pulled out his wallet.

"I'll get it," she told him.

His eyes darted down to her and he shook his head. "I invited you, I'll get it."

"This isn't a date."

Her response was greeted with a sneer. "We're well beyond dating, don't you think?"

That low tone and sexy glimmer in his eye had shivers racing throughout her body. She pulled her coat tighter around her waist and stepped aside as he paid. Once he was done, she turned and moved around the stone fireplace and found the leather sofa in the back unoccupied. There wasn't anyone in this area, actually, and Sara wondered if being alone with Ian was a good idea or not. But they were still in a public place and what else could happen? They'd already slept together.

Sara removed her coat and placed it over the arm of the sofa before she took a seat.

"Relax." She patted the cushion beside her. "The

weather is fine and they will bring our order. So sit down before you give me anxiety."

Ian raked a hand over the back of his neck and Sara wondered what could be bother him that much. The weather? It was just a few snowflakes. Certainly nothing to get worked up about. December in Kentucky was unpredictable so those who lived here just learned to roll with whatever Mother Nature handed them.

"Ian. Relax," she repeated.

Finally, he glanced to her and nodded. He took a seat, but not too close as he remained on the edge of the cushion with his elbows resting on his knees.

"You were more relaxed back at the distillery," she told him. "Maybe leaving wasn't the best idea."

"I'm fine," he assured her. "Snow just makes me nervous."

"I can tell. If you're not comfortable driving when we leave, I can. I've never lived anywhere else, so I'm used to this."

"No," he insisted. "You're not driving. It's far too dangerous."

Dangerous? That's not at all what she would use to describe the conditions, but before she could say anything else, the barista brought their drinks and scones.

Sara met the eyes of the server. "Thank you, Megan."

"Sure thing, Sara. Let me know if you guys need anything else."

"Oh, there is a to-go order I'd like to place," Sara added. Might as well get some items to take with her to snack on later.

Once Megan took the order and Ian and Sara were alone again, Sara reached for her scone, which already had her mouth watering.

"Are you always so personable?"

Ian's question caught her off guard as she glanced to him. "Personable?" she asked.

"Calling people by their names," he explained. "You did that at the bourbon bar and here. I assume you're just as chipper and energetic with your clients and staff."

Sara couldn't help but laugh. "I try to make people around me feel comfortable and important."

Ian merely grunted.

"Clearly you work too much by yourself if that's a foreign concept," she added.

"Not so much foreign," he corrected, reaching for his black coffee. "You and I just have entirely different views of how to accomplish success."

Sara rolled his words around inside her head and finally nodded. "I suppose you're right. We're both good at what we do. You're just disgruntled and I'm positive."

She broke off a piece of her scone, but not before catching his narrowed side-eye.

"I'm not disgruntled," he corrected. "I'd call it realistic."

"Jaded."

"Experienced."

Sara chewed her bite and figured going in circles with Ian wouldn't get either of them anywhere. She enjoyed her scone while Ian sipped on his coffee. They might be total opposites when it came to their outlook and paths they traveled to success, but the underlying physical similarities couldn't be dismissed.

"My mother used to make scones."

Ian's words were so low she barely heard them. When she glanced his way, he was staring at the pastry and she had a feeling he'd just been caught thinking out loud. She wanted to know more, wanted to use this opening he'd presented her to jump straight through and learn all she could about such an intriguing man.

"Did she love to bake?" Sara asked softly, shifting in her seat to face him.

He blinked and took a sip of his coffee. Sara wondered if he'd shut this conversation down before it could truly get started. But to her surprise, he went on.

"She actually ran a bakery in my hometown. Helen's Bakery. She named it after my grandmother who taught her to bake."

"Sounds like a family trait. Did you pick up any skills?"

Ian shook his head. "I tried, but the only thing I found to excel at in the kitchen is eating. My poor mom tried to teach me, but I never got the hang of recipes."

"She must be proud of you for your accomplishments, though."

His lips thinned and the muscle in his jaw ticked. "She passed when I was a teen."

Sara's heart clenched at the sorrow lacing his voice. She knew that hurt, that indescribable pain that came from losing the one person in your life who held your whole world together.

"Losing such an important part of yourself is difficult," she told him. "And I obviously never knew your mother, but I bet she'd be proud of the man you are today."

Ian stared at her, his brows raised just a fraction, but enough to give Sara insight to the fact he'd never had that thought before.

"You've done so much in your career," she added. "Any mother would be honored to have you as her son."

"I guess she would be," he murmured after a moment. "But we're supposed to be discussing you and your business."

"No reason we can't throw a bit of your backstory in there as well." Sara reached for her hot mocha and held on to the warm cup. "Maybe I'd like to know more."

Ian shook his head. "No reason for you to learn more about me. You already know more than most people."

"Wow, you really are a recluse."

"You say that as if it's a bad thing."

Sara couldn't help but laugh. "It sounds lonely and depressing."

"I've been pretty damn happy most of my life."

Sara stared at his dark eyes and he might say the right words, but there was no masking that pain. She recognized heartache.

"You look miserable," she told him. "I can see why you're so great with words on paper, but in person, you can't lie."

"We're supposed to be talking about you," he countered.

"You also can't change the subject."

"I can."

Sara didn't want to argue. She believed him when he said she knew more than most people. There wasn't a doubt in her mind that he held all of his emotions and memories close to his chest. Perhaps that's why he hid behind his computer. Maybe he got into the journalism field so he could focus on other people's problems or lives instead of dealing with his own.

"You're over there trying to figure out my mind," Ian stated after a moment. "Don't waste your time."

"Maybe I like trying to figure other people out," she retorted. "Maybe you *need* someone to figure you out to help you move on from the hurt."

He sat his mug down before sliding his arm across the back of the sofa and leaning further into her. Those coal-like eyes held her still, her breath catching in her throat. Clearly she'd struck a nerve, but that's what happened when too many feelings were suppressed.

"I don't need anything or anyone," he growled. "One night of sex doesn't give you any power over me or the pass to gain access into my world."

Those words were harsh, but Sara had thick skin. She'd pushed and poked, wanting to know more, but she'd gone too far. Still, that didn't give him the right to be hateful.

"Our night together has nothing to do with why I was asking," she defended, still holding his gaze. "I know what it's like to hurt and to not know how to express myself. I know what it's like to lose someone who meant everything, and I sure as hell know that closing in on yourself is not the answer."

He stared for another moment before easing back.

"We've already established we tend to go through life on different paths."

"Maybe this date wasn't the best idea," she suggested.

"It's not a date," he corrected. "We both needed out of that space and to clear our minds."

Sara snorted. "Do you feel better?"

Ian's lips twitched as if he was holding back a smile. "The coffee was good."

"If you're not eating that scone, I will."

Now he did smile as he gestured to the pastry. "Go right ahead. I haven't had one in years."

Since his mother died—at least she assumed that's the rest of the sentence he didn't say out loud. Before Sara could respond or even snag the scone from the dainty plate, her cell chimed from her bag.

"Excuse me."

She turned and opened her purse to find her cell. She'd had a call this morning with the private investigator and there might be a tip on the location of her biological father. She'd been shaken up, knowing she was just one step closer to discovering his identity...*her* identity.

Did the PI already have an answer? Would Sara be able to make that life-altering decision of whether or not she wanted to meet the man? Did he even know she existed?

There were so many questions and she couldn't even grasp all the thoughts swirling around in her mind.

The cell chimed once again.

"Are you getting that?" Ian asked, pulling her from her thoughts.

Sara's hand shook as she reached for the phone and shot Ian a glance. Her eyes darted to the screen, only to see Delilah's name. A wave of disappointment rippled through her, but she had to be patient. She'd gone over thirty years not knowing who her father was. A few more days or even months wouldn't matter.

"Hey, Dee," she answered. "What's up?"

"Where are you?"

"Rise and Grind. Why? Need a mocha latte?"

"I'd love one, but the roads are getting kind of bad all of a sudden. I heard some customers talking and Cam just came by to give me a lift home. We're going to have to close early and I didn't know where you were."

Sara came to her feet and walked toward the front of the coffee shop. Sure enough, those flurries were coming faster and fatter than before. Cars were creeping by on the street. She recalled how nervous Ian had been when there had only been a little skiff of snow.

"I'm with Ian in his rental, but I can just have him take me home."

"Okay. Be careful. Cam and I will shut things down here."

"Thanks, and you be careful, too."

Sara had no idea the weather was supposed to take a turn, but clearly she'd been preoccupied arguing with Ian. She battled between wanting to wring his neck or rip off his clothes. There was no in between.

After she disconnected the call, she made her way back to Ian, who had a worried look on his face. Those thick brows were drawn in and his eyes locked onto hers.

"Something wrong?" he asked as she approached.

"No, but we should head out." Sara picked up the scone plate and decided she needed a to-go box. "Let me grab my other order on the way out, too."

"Is there a rush?"

Sara shrugged as she grabbed her purse and shouldered it. "The weather took a turn, so we should probably head home before the roads become too bad."

Ian muttered a curse under his breath and helped her gather their dishes to take to the bin next to the counter. Sara grabbed a box from the barista, now filled with sandwiches and scones, and shrugged into her coat, wishing she would have thought to get her scarf and gloves. She'd been too surprised that Ian demanded a field trip, her thought process hadn't been working right.

"I'll drive," she told him as they reached the door. She reached her hand out toward him. "Keys."

Ian jerked his attention from the glass doors to her. "Hell no. My name is on that rental. I'll drive."

"Listen, you live at the beach and I've lived here my whole life. I swear, if something happens to your vehicle, I'll take care of it, but I'm used to this weather."

He looked like he wanted to argue, but she raised her brows and held his gaze, silently daring him to keep arguing. Why was it that was all they could do besides sex? The man could be infuriating, but she was not backing down.

"Where are we going?" he asked. "My house is on the other side of town and the distillery is too far with those curvy roads."

Yeah, she'd already thought of all that…which only left one option.

"We're going to my house."

Nine

What the hell was actually happening here?

Ian barely resisted the urge to grip the door or the console as Sara maneuvered through the streets heading toward her home. She claimed her house was the closest of their options, but they'd been driving ten minutes and he was more than ready to get out before he embarrassed himself by having a panic attack.

The SUV slid as Sara took a curve and Ian's breath caught in his throat.

"We're good," she assured him in that soothing tone of hers. "There's a sheet of ice beneath that fresh snow from when we had rain and then the temps dropped. The snow is actually helping to give us some traction."

He didn't say anything—he *couldn't* say anything. Flashes of another freak snowstorm with another woman driving threatened to consume him. Hell, those images *were* consuming him. He needed to get out of this vehicle now.

"Almost there," she murmured.

Ian didn't know how she remained so damn calm when they were fishtailing down the road. One jerk of the wheel or one car sliding toward them could alter everything and put them both at risk.

"Are you going to hyperventilate?"

Ian shook his head, still unable to find words. He wanted to close his eyes, but part of him felt the need to know what was happening around him. Not that he had any control here…nor had he the night his mother was killed.

That's what terrified him most of all. The lack of control and no way to undo the damage of his past. He just had to live with it every day, like a lead weight he'd been carrying around for years that he couldn't shake off.

"We're here."

Sara eased into a tree-lined drive. The path had no tracks and seemed long, so long that he couldn't see the house yet.

"You're safe," she told him. "Even if we slide off the driveway, we're just in my yard."

Ian released a breath he hadn't realized he'd been holding. He kept his eyes fixed out the windshield and finally spotted a two-story dark blue home with a stone porch. The charming style sent a wave of calm through him. He didn't know why the sight of her house settled him, but it did. They were done traveling for now and he'd worry about how to get to his own place later.

After Sara pulled into the garage, she killed the engine and shifted to face him.

"I knew you didn't like the weather earlier, but I had no idea this was a true phobia."

"It's not a phobia."

She tipped her head and leveled his stare. "I realize you don't like to admit you might actually have human emotions, but there's nothing wrong with being afraid of something."

"I'm fine."

Could this get any more humiliating?

Sara let out the most unladylike growl and jerked the door handle. She snagged the to-go box from the center console and hopped out of the vehicle and promptly marched right inside her home. With the door into her house standing wide open, he assumed she was going to let him inside, even though she was clearly frustrated.

He wasn't about to admit his nagging worries to a virtual stranger. He still wanted to preserve his pride and those deepest fears.

Ian made his way into the house and closed the door behind him. The utility room was neat and tidy with labels for everything from dirty laundry to the detergent. He wasn't at all surprised that Sara liked things nice and orderly.

He made his way on into the kitchen where she stood at the large island. Her palms were flat on the granite with the to-go box between her hands. She stared out the back window as fat flakes continued to swirl. Being alone with her in her house might not have been his first choice, but he sure as hell knew his anxiety wouldn't have allowed him to make it all the way to the other side of town to his house.

"I'm afraid of being alone."

Sara's soft words slid between them as she kept her eyes fixed away from him.

"You live alone, though, right?" he asked.

Now she blinked and redirected her focus. "I do, but my fear is of always being alone. I bought this house with every intention of filling it with a family. My family. Each year that goes by, I wonder if I was too optimistic."

Ian never thought of being alone or that he'd likely be that way forever. The idea of giving a piece of himself to anyone and opening up the possibilities of pain and loss again wasn't worth the risk.

But someone like Sara would want that familial lifestyle. He could see her expertly juggling a high-profile career with a husband and children.

An unexpected pang of jealousy hit him at the idea of some faceless man in her life. Ian already hated the bastard. How did one night of passion make him have such irrational thoughts? Hadn't he told her that their night didn't give a pass into his life? The same should be true for hers because there was no way in hell he would fill that role for Sara. No, he was leaving town as soon as the article was done and he could go back to the warmth of Miami where he could start the next chapter in his career.

At least, that was the plan. But it sounded so... cold.

"You're still young." Ian came to stand on the other side of the island, needing that barrier between them. "There's plenty of time to meet 'the one' and have a family."

Sara chewed on her lip as if trying to figure out a timeline. She shrugged from her coat and hung it over the high-back barstool.

"Let me have your coat," she told him. "I'm not sure how long we'll be hunkered down here, but hopefully the plow and the salt trucks will come through and you can get back to your place this evening."

Yeah, because the alternative would be spending the night here and he knew full well how that would turn out. He prided himself on being in control in all aspects of his life, but when it came to Sara, she flipped that switch to Off and he was at her mercy.

Did she even know? There was an innocent power she held and he doubted she had any clue that she could have any man she wanted. That family she so desired? All she'd have to do is snap her fingers and any man would come running into her life, ready to give her everything she'd ever dreamed of.

Not him, but any other man.

If he were looking to settle down, Sara would be perfect wife material. She understood the work ethic, she had a drive for success and she valued those close in her life.

Added to all of that, she was sexy as hell and he didn't think he'd ever find a better lover.

Suddenly hotter, Ian removed his coat and walked around the island to hang it on the stool next to Sara's. His arm brushed hers as he shifted. Ian's fingers curled around the back of the stool as he grappled. He prided himself on dominating every situation, yet he couldn't get a handle on his own emotions. He was still too raw, too vulnerable from the circumstances that led him to her house. He had to get that day, those images, out of his mind if he was going to be able to stay strong during his unexpected visit.

"Do you want to tell me about earlier?" she asked gently, her dark eyes boring into his.

He'd swear she could see right into his soul, and perhaps that's what she was trying to do, but he needed to keep that door shut.

"We already moved on from that topic," he reminded her.

"Being vulnerable isn't a problem." She reached out and laid her hand over his. "I'm a pretty good listener and I wouldn't tell anyone. We all have secrets and sometimes the best way to move on is to get the weight off your chest."

He stared at her, knowing she believed every word she said. But that simple touch of her hand clicked something inside him and the dead last thing he wanted to do was chat about the past that still haunted him twenty years later.

Ian jerked his hand from beneath hers and took a step back. "I can wait out in the truck until it's safe to go."

When he started to walk by, Sara grabbed hold of his elbow. His forearm brushed the edge of her breast and he noted the pulse on her neck quickening. The intensity threatened to consume him, to push him even further into her world, and he couldn't mentally afford to get lost in this trap.

Sex the other night had muddled everything since they'd met initially in her office. They'd started every aspect of their working and professional relationship off on the wrong foot and he'd been scrambling to regain his footing since.

"This is a bad idea," he growled, glancing from her hand to her face.

"We're just talking. Isn't that what we're supposed to be doing anyway? That is why you're here."

Wasn't she cute, messing with his mind like this? He couldn't fall for her charm or her compassion or her sex appeal. Why did she have to be everything all wrapped up in one neat, tidy package?

"Listen, we'll work on the interview if that makes

FREE BOOKS GIVEAWAY

GET UP TO FOUR FREE BOOKS & TWO FREE GIFTS WORTH OVER $20!

We pay for everything!

See Details Inside

Dear Reader,

I am writing to announce the launch of a huge **FREE BOOKS GIVEAWAY**... and to let you know that YOU are entitled to choose up to FOUR fantastic books that WE pay for.

Try **Harlequin® Desire** books featuring the worlds of the American elite with juicy plot twists, delicious sensuality and intriguing scandal.

Try **Harlequin Presents® Larger-Print** books featuring the glamourous lives of royals and billionaires in a world of exotic locations, where passion knows no bounds.

Or **TRY BOTH!**

In return, we ask just one favor: Would you please participate in our brief Reader Survey? We'd love to hear from you.

This FREE BOOKS GIVEAWAY means that your introductory shipment is completely free, <u>even the shipping</u>! If you decide to continue, you can look forward to curated monthly shipments of brand-new books from your selected series, always at a discount off the cover price! <u>Plus you can cancel any time</u>. Who could pass up a deal like that?

Sincerely

Pam Powers

Pam Powers
For Harlequin Reader Service

Complete the survey below and return it today to receive up to 4 FREE BOOKS and FREE GIFTS guaranteed!

FREE BOOKS GIVEAWAY
Reader Survey

1
Do you prefer stories with happy endings?

◯ YES ◯ NO

2
Do you share your favorite books with friends?

◯ YES ◯ NO

3
Do you often choose to read instead of watching TV?

◯ YES ◯ NO

YES! Please send me my Free Rewards, consisting of **2 Free Books from each series I select** and **Free Mystery Gifts**. I understand that I am under no obligation to buy anything, no purchase necessary see terms and conditions for details.

❏ **Harlequin Desire®** (225/326 HDL GRQJ)
❏ **Harlequin Presents® Larger-Print** (176/376 HDL GRQJ)
❏ **Try Both** (225/326 & 176/376 HDL GRQU)

FIRST NAME

LAST NAME

ADDRESS

APT.#

CITY

STATE/PROV.

ZIP/POSTAL CODE

EMAIL ❏ Please check this box if you would like to receive newsletters and promotional emails from Harlequin Enterprises ULC and its affiliates. You can unsubscribe anytime.

HD/HP-122-FBG22

you more comfortable." She dropped her hand, but didn't move away. "We can settle in the living room and you can ask whatever else you need to know."

Ian laughed. "We're not even close to everything I want to know."

Sara's smile widened and another kick of lust hit his gut. Yeah, being alone with this woman was nothing but trouble and he'd originally thought she was naive and had no clue…now he was starting to believe she knew precisely what she was doing and she was driving him out of his ever-loving mind.

"You could say that Elise is definitely the brains of the group," Sara stated, tucking her feet up beside her on the sofa. "Delilah is the guarded one, but she's softened a little since getting back together with Cam."

"And they were divorced?" Ian asked from the opposite end of the couch as he typed notes into his phone.

"Not yet. Nobody had signed the papers." Sara sighed. "Those two were always meant to be together. They met and had a whirlwind affair and next thing I knew, they were getting married. I guess they just knew from the start."

Ian sat his cell down and stretched his arm along the back cushion. "Delilah said Elise met her husband at Angel's Share and then something about getting locked in the basement."

Sara couldn't help but laugh. "Yes, Antonio came

to the States to look for distilleries and wineries to partner with for his family's chain of restaurants in Spain. Long story short, he and Elise got locked in the cellar of the castle together during a rainstorm and now they're on their honeymoon."

Ian's eyes widened. "You ladies work fast."

There went that pang of remorse once again. "Two of us, anyway."

Maybe she wouldn't marry. Perhaps she'd be like Milly and just care for others. Milly had a happy, satisfying life…didn't she? Sara never recalled her mother wanting to marry or have a serious relationship. She dated very rarely, but with raising three girls and making sure their lives were enriched, maybe Milly just didn't have the time.

"Don't go there," Ian scolded. "Stop worrying about when you'll get married. It will happen if that's what you want. I firmly believe you don't let obstacles get in your way."

Sara blinked and pulled herself back to the moment. "I definitely don't, but I was just thinking about Milly."

"That's your mother who just passed."

Sara nodded. "She never married. I never thought about that until now, that she was always so busy making us happy and pushing us to fulfill our dreams. I just wonder what her dreams were."

"Maybe that was her dream," he countered. "To see her children happy."

The thought warmed Sara and she smiled. "You sound as if you knew her."

"It's easy to see the type of woman she was when there are three successful, powerful women living out her legacy."

Damn. He did have a way with words. Who knew this interview would be a balm to her wounded soul?

Not only his words, but his presence. It had been a long time since a man sat on her living room sofa and talked. Even if this moment was by chance because of the weather, she didn't mind. The soft glow from her Christmas tree and mantel lights gave the room an even cozier vibe. There was a content blanket that seemed to cover her right now and she couldn't help but wish this moment would never end.

"So why a distillery?" Ian asked. "You said yesterday the male-dominated bourbon industry is the main reason you three wanted to dive into it. Tell me why."

"We wanted to bring something different, yet something that we knew would be a success. Kentucky loves bourbon and they love rich history. Opening a distillery in an old, abandoned castle seemed like a no-brainer."

As he put notes into his phone, Sara went on. "I can rephrase that if you want something more eloquent for your piece."

Those thin lips quirked again. She couldn't help but stare…and remember. He'd been such a giving lover. Her desire for him was stronger now than ever before. Seeing him humanized earlier had really added a surprising element to all the layers that seemed to make up this mystifying man.

"You're staring."

Sara shrugged. "You're attractive. What else do you want me to do? Close my eyes?"

Ian's bark of laughter caught her off guard. She wasn't going to apologize for enjoying the view. Clearly she wouldn't be doing more than that because he'd made it clear they were, as Dee stated, "a one and done." Granted everything about this was unique and completely out of the norm, but Sara couldn't help but wonder how they'd be now that they knew each other even more.

Ian might not be "the one" she was waiting for, but she had to live her life and enjoy herself until that person came into her world.

"What made you take me back to your house the other night?"

She hadn't meant to ask that, but now that the words were out, she wasn't sorry. Because she'd gotten a good glimpse of the man and his personality, and taking a strange woman home was not in his character.

"I rarely deny myself anything and it had been too long since a woman intrigued me the way you did."

Well…that was eye-opening and a useful nugget of information.

"I expected you to fully dodge that question," she admitted.

The fire in her gas fireplace kicked on, immediately giving her cozy living room those warm, inviting vibes—not to mention romantic. As if she needed more of a push to romanticize this entire situation. She was sinking deeper and deeper with a temporary man and Sara knew she had to safeguard her heart and her mind, but she was having a difficult time grasping that concept.

"I believe in honesty, but I don't always answer when I'm not comfortable."

"And you're comfortable with me?" she asked.

"Surprisingly, I am."

Another useful piece to lock away. She was chipping away at his steely exterior and those guarded walls.

Sara pulled her old cardigan tighter around her and rested her head on the back cushion. Before she realized it, a yawn escaped and she covered her mouth in a vain attempt to mask her exhaustion.

"Go lie down," he told her. "I'm fine here."

"I'm not just taking a nap with a guest in my house," she scoffed.

"Why not? It's not like we've done anything normal since meeting, anyway."

"True," she agreed. "But I'm fine. I think my body is used to just going at warp speed, so when I'm still for too long, it thinks I should be asleep."

"Maybe—"

Sara's celled chimed from the pocket of her old sweater. She'd changed before they'd settled into the living room in her favorite leggings, Milly's cardigan and a pair of fuzzy socks. Definitely not the sexy look she'd given Ian on their first encounter.

She pulled the phone out and glanced to the screen. Her heart clenched as the name stared back at her.

"I need to take this."

Ian waved her on. "Go ahead."

With a shaky hand, Sara gripped her cell and came to her feet. She needed to have this conversation in private because she had no clue what information she was about to receive or how she would react.

She tapped the screen as she moved into her office and closed the double doors.

"Hello."

"Sara, I have something."

Her heart beat faster at the words she'd been waiting to hear for a while now.

"What is it? You found my father?"

"I found him."

Sara's knees weakened and she sank right to the floor. She concentrated on what her investigator continued to say at the same time as she tried to breathe deeply and not pass out.

Since the moment she and her sisters had discovered they were actually half sisters and not just the very best of friends, Sara had been searching for her birth father. Elise hadn't wanted to find hers and Delilah was still on the fence about meeting the man who'd fathered her after Cam tracked him down.

But Sara wanted to know. She had that yearning to get her own backstory. Yes, she had an amazing life with Elise and Delilah and she'd had the best upbringing with Milly…but there was still a void she wanted to fill.

"He does have a family," the investigator went on. "I was wrong about his name being James, though. Your father's name is Trenton Mills and he lives in Knoxville. He's a schoolteacher there and his son just graduated from high school last year. His wife is the principal at the same school. They seem to be a very tight-knit family from everything I've uncovered."

Family. That word meant so many different things and looked so many different ways. Yet there was love at the root.

"I wonder if he even knows about me," she murmured.

"I never approached him, but I can do more digging or I can hand over all I know along with his contact information."

Sara closed her eyes and attempted to push back the unshed tears. Swallowing the burn in her throat, she replied, "I'll take the information, please. I can take it from here."

"I had a feeling you'd say that. I'll email everything now."

"Thank you. Seriously. I can't thank you enough."

"I'm always glad when I help someone."

Sara ended the call and immediately went to her

email. She kept refreshing until minutes later, the file showed up and she instantly dug into it.

There were photographs. So many images, and she wanted to devour them all at once. She'd definitely pull these up on her computer later and print everything out, but she couldn't wait, so the small phone screen would have to suffice.

She scrolled through quickly, then went back to the beginning and stared at each one, dissecting for any glimpse of a similarity. She definitely had her father's eyes and mouth...so did her brother.

A cry caught in her throat as the first tear slipped down her cheek. She had a brother who likely didn't know she existed. For all Sara knew, her father had no idea, either.

Was it right for her to be so selfish and disrupt his life? Would he want to know she was out there? How did someone so successful and grounded get involved with a habitual drug user like Sara's biological mother? There were still so many questions, but all she wanted to know was if he would want the truth about her. That's all that mattered now.

She'd have to talk to Dee and Elise because she needed their support more than ever, but she was ready to open this new chapter in her life book.

Ten

Ian tapped on the office door. When the wood gave beneath his knuckles, he eased the door open and spotted Sara on the floor. She turned to look up at him and those red-rimmed eyes and tear tracks down her cheeks had him bursting in and immediately at her side.

"What's wrong? What happened?" he demanded.

He sank to his knees and glanced to her phone. She'd been looking at images of a family he didn't recognize, but he wanted to know what the hell happened from her taking a call almost an hour ago, until now when she'd clearly been having an emotional moment on the floor.

"Oh, my word." Her damp eyes widened as she

shoved her cell back into her sweater pocket. "I forgot all about you."

"Well, that never helps a man's ego," he joked, hoping to lighten the mood. Ian shifted to sit more comfortably at her side on the rug. "Is everything all right? Did you get bad news?"

Sara shook her head. "I got amazing news, but I just don't know how to process everything. And I was so wrapped up in everything, I lost track of time and touch with reality. I'm so sorry, Ian."

Relief settled inside him. "Don't be sorry. I started to worry when you didn't come back and then when I saw you on the floor crying... Damn it. Don't scare me like that."

Sara patted the side of his face, her fingertips brushing his scar.

"See? You do care and aren't so coldhearted."

That touch, so simple and playful, yet so arousing, struck a nerve he'd thought for sure he'd severed.

Ian reached up and grabbed her hand, curling his fingers around her delicate ones. Sara's eyes widened, and her mouth dropped open as she continued to stare at him.

"Is that how you see me?" he asked. "Cold?"

"I— Well. No."

Damn right he wasn't cold. He was so hot right now, he should have waited in his vehicle like he suggested hours ago, but here he was alone and on the floor with Sara...the woman who wouldn't get out of his mind. Even when he was alone, she was there, always in the forefront and demanding his attention.

"Are you going to kiss me?" she whispered, her gaze dropping to his lips.

"Is that what you want, Sara? You want me to kiss you? To make you remember the other night?"

She inched closer. "I want you to make the other night happen again."

Hell. There was no way he could deny her...or himself. They'd danced around this moment since they reunited in her office. But she was vulnerable. Whatever happened with that phone call had taken her to a new place and he didn't want to be a regret.

Ian pulled her hand away from his face and tugged her closer until she fell against his chest. He searched her eyes for any sign of doubt, but only saw desire.

"Are you using me to forget your trouble?" he asked.

"Maybe. Is that a problem?"

Not a problem, but he was surprised that there was a sliver of disappointment. He never wanted connections or ties to anyone or anything. He sure as hell wasn't looking for any of that now, either. But something about her being so casual confused him.

Perhaps he was just caught off guard because she was unlike any woman he'd ever met. Maybe what he needed at this point in his life was a simple, sexy distraction, and Sara wasn't asking for anything more...at least not from him.

"You're thinking an awfully long time," Sara stated as she started to ease back.

Ian held tight and rested his forehead against hers.

"Occupational hazard," he explained. "I process everything before acting."

A smile danced around her pale pink lips. "And did you process everything on Saturday when you took me back to your place?"

Ian couldn't help but chuckle. "I sure as hell processed everything about you and my decision."

"Then I guess it's decided." Sara moved her hand from his and looped her arms around his neck as she crawled into his lap. "We need to make sure you made the right decision then and now."

Oh, he was pretty damn sure he'd made the right decision both times, but he was done talking. Whatever was going on in Sara's personal life had nothing to do with him and if she needed the escape from reality, he'd be the one offering it. He couldn't explain the territorial tendency when it came to this woman, but he wasn't about to explore those unwanted emotions now.

"And maybe you need to use me as well," she added. "You were pretty stressed earlier. There's nowhere to go for now, so…"

No. There was nowhere to go and he was going to take full advantage of this snowstorm.

Ian slid his hands around Sara's waist, easing his fingertips beneath the hem of her tank. Her warmth

penetrated him in ways he'd never experienced before her. How could just one simple touch be both
erotic and soothing? He was here in this moment
for the physical aspect of this relationship...noth-
ing more. He couldn't afford more.

When Sara arched into him and dropped her head
back, Ian seized the opportunity. He'd been dying
to taste her since the last time they were together.
He trailed his lips over the smooth column of her
throat until he reached her chin. Sara shifted and
met his lips with her own as she threaded her fingers through his hair.

Liquid fire. That's the only term Ian could use
to describe the way Sara reacted in his arms. No
doubt she was good for a bruised, battered soul, not
to mention pretty damn nice for his ego.

But she was more. Much more than he'd ever
admit out loud...so he squelched the thoughts before he could get too carried away. There were so
many layers to intimacy, and he only wanted the
superficial.

"You're thinking too hard again," she murmured
against his lips. "Relax."

"This floor is damn hard," he grunted. "I'm not
young anymore."

Sara laughed and pulled away as she came to
her feet. When she extended her hand and smiled
down at him, Ian's heart did a flip that irritated the
hell out of him. There was no room for heart flips
or any other bonding emotion.

Ian reached for her hand and rose, but immediately lifted her into his arms. Sara's playful squeal reminded him of just how opposite they were. At first he was confused by their differences, but she was starting to grow on him...which could prove to be dangerous.

The plush, pale yellow couch in the corner would have to work. He wasn't about to use a hard surface like the desk or the floor. She deserved better, but the bed was out. For one thing, he didn't know where her bedroom was, and for another, crossing that threshold would take them to a level he would never be ready for.

His eyes landed on the couch and he nearly groaned.

"What do you have so many damn throw pillows for?"

Sara locked her ankles behind his back and circled his neck with her arms as she glanced across the room to the silver-and-white pillows, all with Christmas patterns or some holiday wording.

"Because I'm a woman and I like pretty accessories. Don't ask questions. Just go with it."

Of course she liked pretty things. She was simple in that way and wanted her world to be festive and fun. He never knew that manner of thinking and had never really gotten to know anyone like that, either.

He'd known Sara less than a week and she'd already changed something inside him. Who the hell knew the person he'd be once he finally left Benton Springs?

Ian dropped Sara onto the pillow-covered couch and stood over her. Damn, but she was breathtaking with her dark hair spread all around her and her smiling lips swollen from his kisses.

"I love when you look at me like that."

Ian stilled. How had he been looking at her? What could she possibly have seen?

He wasn't about to ask because he didn't want to know the answer…especially when she tacked on the *L* word to the sentence.

Ian unbuttoned his vest and let it fall to the floor. He started working the buttons on his shirt, moving slowly to enjoy Sara's watchful gaze. He couldn't deny he thoroughly enjoyed having her look at him like he was the only thing in the world that mattered. He didn't have that in his personal life. Didn't know he wanted something like that until now.

An unwanted emotional tug pulled at his heart and Ian knew he'd have to work like hell not to lose control. He had no idea how Sara could have this hold over him in such a short amount of time and she likely had no clue the power she possessed.

"There you go thinking again," she murmured as she sat up. "Those worry lines between your brows get even deeper. What has you so bothered?"

You.

"The fact that you're still wearing so many clothes." He ridded himself of his shirt and went

to the buckle of his belt. "Or am I the only one getting ready for this party?"

Sara cocked her head. "I am enjoying the show,
but I'm starting to feel overdressed."

She took off her cardigan, then reached for the
hem of her tank, keeping her gaze locked onto his.
Ian continued to shed his clothes as he stared down
at her, but when she came to her feet, Ian had to take
a step back.

As much as he enjoyed having her half-dressed,
he wanted her completely bare. The urgency of his
need and ache had him reaching for her pants and
helping her out of them and her undergarments in
record time.

Ian slid his hands over the flare of her bare hips
and settled in that dip in her waist as he stepped toward her. Her breasts grazed his chest and another
punch of arousal coursed through him.

"Protection?" she asked, looping her arms
around his neck. "I don't have any. It's not like I
bring men back here."

For reasons he didn't want to explore, Ian liked
knowing she didn't have anyone regular in her life.
That territorial feeling came over him again. He
wanted to keep her all to himself...but that wasn't
possible. They lived in two different worlds and had
completely different outlooks on life.

All they had was here and now.

"I don't have any with me," he told her. "I didn't
think I'd end up here when I set out this morning."

Sara pursed her lips and another wave of need pumped through him.

"I'm clean," she murmured. "But if you want to stop, I—"

Ian captured her lips. No way could he stop now unless she put on the brakes.

His grip on her waist tightened as he pulled her body flush with his and deepened the kiss. Carefully, Ian lifted her off the floor and turned. When the back of his knees bumped the edge of the sofa, Ian eased down. Sara straddled his lap and settled over him as she pulled from the kiss and stared down.

"I'm clean, too," he assured her. "I'd never do anything to hurt you."

And he'd never wanted to be with someone without protection, either. Sara was doing something to him, something he couldn't reason with in his own mind.

Sara's smile spread across her face as she slowly joined their bodies, all the while keeping her heavy-lidded gaze on his.

The little minx knew just how potent she was. Clearly she wasn't as innocent as he'd thought and that fact made her even more desirable than before. The juxtaposition of her personalities was surprising and maybe even a little challenging. No matter what version of Sara he was presented with, he couldn't resist.

The moment they were joined as one, Sara dropped her head back and arched her body. He remembered from the other evening how sexy she looked in this pose, but he wanted something else. There was so much more to explore with her and now that they had nowhere to go and could take their time, he wanted to do just that.

Ian banded an arm around her waist and shifted until he had her flat on her back. He loomed over her as she locked her ankles behind his back. All of that dark hair fanned around her, her eyes had a hunger in them that he knew matched his own, and then she reached for him. Her hands framed his face as her lips parted, silently urging him to kiss her.

He gripped the arm of the sofa just above her head and reached back to grab hold of her thigh. Then he moved. His hips jerked against hers and he covered her mouth. He wanted all of her at the same time. He wanted to consume everything within her and be all she thought of, all she wanted.

Sara's body danced with his and her urgency was apparent as she moaned into his mouth. Ian pulled her leg a little higher, giving her a more intense experience. She tore her mouth from his and cried out, bowing back and trembling all around him.

Ian stilled, wanting to feel her come completely undone around him. Coupled with seeing her passion explode, Ian had to use all of his self-control to let her finish. He didn't want to miss a single moment of her pleasure.

The moment Sara's body started to settle, he moved again. Faster this time as he worked toward his own release. Her fingertips trailed over his lips, down his throat and over his bare chest. His body couldn't take another second and he welcomed the rush.

Sara murmured something as her hands continued to roam, but he couldn't make it out. His desire had been too strong, his release too intense, to concentrate on anything else.

The moment he came down from the high, Ian rested his elbows on either side of Sara's head and smoothed her hair from her face. She stared up at him with her heart in her eyes and Ian had to close his and pretend he didn't just see straight into her soul.

"I'm glad you're here," she whispered.

Yeah. He couldn't say the words, but he was, too.

Now how the hell was he supposed to deal with that nugget of information? He didn't belong, he didn't *want* to belong, anywhere. Yet here he was, sliding right into a world he didn't want.

Eleven

"So what comes after this project?"

Sara stretched her legs out on the sofa and propped her feet on Ian's lap. They'd never made it out of her office, but they were both now wearing his clothes. He'd put back on his dress pants, but left them unbuttoned, and she'd thrown on his shirt. She'd be lying if she didn't admit she loved the smell of him on her. It took all of her willpower not to turn her nose into the collar and inhale deeply.

"When you leave Benton Springs, what will you do next?" she added. "You seem to travel the world, from all I've seen with your articles."

Ian rested his hand on her ankle and curled those long fingers around her foot. When he started to massage, Sara nearly groaned, but refrained from that as well. She wanted to learn even more about him. The snow was still coming down and she'd sent off texts checking on the employees and the distillery. Everything was under control, so the only thing that needed her attention right now was Ian.

The information about her father wouldn't be going anywhere and that was something she wanted to share in person with her sisters. Elise would be back from her honeymoon tomorrow, so long as the weather cooperated, and Sara would call a family meeting.

"I'll head back to Miami but I'll be gone from *Elite* before the piece comes out. It's time for a change."

Sara laid her arm across the back cushion and tipped her head. "What makes you want to do something else?"

With a shrug, Ian shifted and faced her. He adjusted her feet in his lap and started back up the massage.

"I'm getting restless," he admitted. "I can't pinpoint why, but my time with *Elite* has come to an end. Nigel opened this door for me years ago and I owe everything to him, but even he agrees that I need to move on."

"So what's your goal? Go back to traveling the world? Take a break from work?"

Ian seemed to be thinking as he studied his hands moving over her bare feet. Maybe he didn't want to share his plans, it wasn't like they had any ties or he owed her any explanation.

"You don't have to tell me," she quickly added. "I'm not trying to be some nosy girlfriend. I mean, I'm not your girlfriend, I'm just—"

"Relax," he told her. "I didn't think you were turning clingy on me. I actually have always wanted to write a book."

"Really? That's amazing."

He gave a nonchalant shrug like writing a book was no big deal.

"I've been all over the world and I'd like to focus on nonfiction from things I've learned from my travels. Who knows, maybe I could write more than one?"

"Do you plan on moving?" she asked.

"I love Miami. It's been my home since I was a teenager."

"After your mom passed?"

Ian's hands stilled on her as his eyes locked onto hers. His silence proved that she had crossed the line into territory he didn't want to get into. Loss could make people close in on themselves and there was no "getting over" such a hardship. But she couldn't help but wonder if he ever talked about her to anybody. Who was in Ian's life that he could confide in or use as a shoulder when needed?

Knowing what she did about Ian, the man likely thought he would be just fine making it through his life by writing about others. He wouldn't need to lean on anyone if there was nothing going on in his own world. Throwing himself into his work and getting wrapped up in each of his projects had likely fulfilled his life all these years.

But he was restless and she knew he was still trying to find something to fill that void his mother had left.

"Forget I asked," she finally stated with a wave of her hand. "We'll talk about something else, but keep up that massaging."

His shoulders relaxed and he resumed rubbing the arch of her foot.

"Would you like to stick around for the gala?" she asked. "Should be a fun night and hopefully no freak snowstorm cancels our plans."

"Today's storm has me ready to head back to Miami as soon as possible, but I still have things to do here." He rested his hands on the top of her feet and leaned forward a bit. "I might be persuaded to stick around and leave after the gala."

Why did that make her so giddy inside? Ian sticking around a little longer didn't mean anything…he was still a temporary fling whether that lasted one week or three weeks. He wasn't staying and they weren't building anything permanent here.

Still, she couldn't help but be excited that she had more time with him, and she fully intended to take advantage of their days together.

"You could always just stay here for the rest of your trip."

When his eyes widened, Sara chewed the inside of her cheek and waited. She hadn't actually meant to say that out loud, but she couldn't take the words back now so she wasn't even going to try to defend them.

"Is that so you can take advantage of me whenever you want?" he asked, a naughty grin dancing around his lips.

Sara shrugged. "Guilty."

At least he wasn't appalled by her request and he hadn't come out and just turned her down...which meant he was thinking about it. Another burst of exhilaration shot through her at the idea of Ian spending his days at the distillery and his nights in her bed.

"You have a spare room?"

His question confused her.

"I have three spare bedrooms. I just assumed—"

"I'll stay, but I won't share your personal room. That's too intimate."

He had a serious issue with any type of bonding or connection, but she would respect his wishes and try to be compassionate about his reasoning.

"Fine by me," she told him. "Once the roads are safe again, we'll go get your stuff."

"We won't have the hot tub," he reminded her.

Sara pulled her feet from his lap and stood. She came to stand before him, then placed one knee on either side of his hips as she straddled his lap.

"Maybe when we go get your things, we can enjoy it one last time," she suggested.

His hands cupped her backside as he rocked her body against his. "You do have the best ideas."

He leaned up to cover her lips with his. She'd never invited a man to live with her before and she didn't know why she had asked Ian, but she wanted to be with him as much as she could for as long as she could. Their time together was dwindling and there was no reason they couldn't have a little fun until their time ran out.

"Well, you look gorgeous and rested."

Elise breezed into the conference room at the distillery and was all smiles. Sara was so happy to see her sisters in love and moving in a new direction. Elise truly did look like she'd rested and relaxed, and that glowing tan only made Sara a tad jealous that her sister had been on some tropical beach.

"I feel refreshed, but still jet-lagged," Elise admitted. "That snowstorm really screwed up our flights, but I guess spending extra days in paradise wasn't a bad thing."

Yeah, Sara hadn't minded those extra days, either, with her new houseguest, but that was definitely not a conversation she was going to get into. There were much more pressing matters to discuss and her heated fling wasn't even in the top three.

"Sorry I'm late." Delilah stepped in right behind Elise. "Cam thought it was a great idea to surprise me with a puppy and I was up all night. Not to mention the shoes I was going to wear had been peed in, so...how's everyone?"

"A puppy! Why didn't you send us any pics?" Sara demanded. "Let me see. What's the name?"

"What's the breed?" Elise chimed in.

Delilah sat her travel coffee mug and her purse on the table and wrapped an arm around Elise. "I'm so glad you're back. You look even more gorgeous and I didn't think that was possible. Anyway, her name is Milly. Is that okay?"

Sara gasped. "Yes, of course! She would have loved that."

Delilah tapped on her cell and scrolled, then turned the phone to face her sisters. "There's several pictures and some videos. She might not sleep and she potties all over the place, but we're working on it and she's just so cute, I can't be mad."

"I can't tell if she's a Lab or what she is," Elise murmured.

"Cam got her from the local animal shelter." Delilah smoothed her dark hair behind her ears and peeked around to see the screen. "He said he'd been thinking of surprising me for a while, but we're usually so busy with our workloads. He's really lightened his cases and spends much more time at home now. He thinks this will be a good segue into a baby."

"What?" Elise's hold on the phone fumbled and Sara caught it. "You guys are thinking of a baby?"

Delilah nodded. "We've talked about it, but nothing is certain. I'm more open to it than I was and the idea of my own family is kind of growing on me."

"You would make a wonderful mother," Sara added. "That's so exciting and I'm going to need to come over and see this pup. She is precious."

"Sure, anytime." Delilah took her cell and sat it down on the table before grabbing her coffee. "So, what's the urgent talk we need to have, Sara? Your text sounded urgent last night."

Sara's stomach knotted as she pulled in a deep breath. Her sisters were so supportive of her decision to find her father, and she knew they'd be happy for her. She was more afraid of what would come once she set out to meet the man.

"My investigator found my father," she told them.

Both of her sisters' mouths dropped open, so Sara hurried on.

"He lives in Knoxville and he has a family of his own." She moved to the head of the table where she had a folder of all the information and photographs she'd been emailed. "I have a good bit here I wanted to share with you guys."

Her sisters were quickly at her side as Sara flipped open the folder. Right there on top was a photograph of her dad, his wife and their son.

"Oh, wow," Elise muttered. "Sara, you look just like him."

"I thought so, too." Emotions threatened to clog her throat, so Sara swallowed and forged ahead. "It's crazy knowing I have another family and that

I actually look like someone. Isn't that silly? I'm excited that I have the same chin as another human being."

"When you're adopted and aren't sure where you came from, that's not silly at all," Elise defended. "You should be excited. So, are you going to call him or try to see him?"

Sara moved to pull out the leather chair and sank into it. Her attention landed back on the photograph and she chewed on her lip while so many thoughts swirled around in her head.

"I do want to reach out, but I don't know the best approach," she confessed. "It's such a life-altering bomb to drop on him. Do I email so he can take time to think of a response? Or do I call so he can put a voice to a person?"

"I would call," Delilah told her. "You know Cam got that information on my father and I've never reached out. I'm not sure I'm going to, but that's just where I'm at. This is your journey so do what's best for you. I think I would make a call because an email is so impersonal."

"Agreed." Elise reached for Sara's hand and gave a reassuring squeeze. "We're here no matter when or how you decide to reach out. This is so exciting, though. I'm really happy for you."

Elise had been adamant that she didn't want to know about her biological father, and Dee had the information, but hadn't done anything with it. Sara couldn't help herself. She had a yearning to learn more about her past and see if there were any more similarities other than physical.

"I guess I'll call, then." Sara blew out a sigh and tried to ignore the nerves swirling around in her belly. "I hope I don't disrupt his life. I mean, what if he knew about me and disregarded the fact that my mother was pregnant?"

Elise shuffled through the papers in the folder, handing some to Delilah as well. Sara waited while her sisters looked over the contents. There wasn't a ton of information to take in, but the necessary basics and much more than she'd ever had before.

"The man has devoted his life to teaching and volunteering with after-school activities," Delilah finally stated. "I'd say he loves children so there's a good chance he didn't know about you."

"I'm so confused, though," Sara replied. "How could someone like this get caught up with someone like our mother? A drug addict who was in and out of rehab for years."

"Our mother did have some clean and sober moments." Elise sat her papers down and took a seat next to Sara. "Maybe that's when they met."

That would have to be the case here. The man in front of Sara seemed to be the total opposite of everything they knew about their biological mother. Sara didn't have ill feelings toward her mother. Sara had never gotten a chance to meet the woman since she passed in prison after being incarcerated for drugs. People made mistakes and Sara just wished her mother had been able to straighten her life out and raise the three girls she'd given birth to.

But Milly had stepped in and adopted all three girls, raising them as her own. Sara had a great childhood with memories that would last her a lifetime.

"Am I being greedy?" she asked. "Wanting more, I mean."

"There's nothing greedy about you." Elise snorted. "And there's nothing wrong with you making a phone call. If he doesn't want to meet you, then you will know. But if he does, that opens up a whole other life for you that could be even more amazing."

That possibility had her anticipation spiking. The hope that she would have more family to love and create memories with had her tearing up.

"Oh, damn it." Delilah went to the accent table near the door and grabbed the box of tissues. "Don't cry because then we will and we all have a full day ahead of us. We're ugly criers, remember?"

Sara laughed and sniffed. "I'm aware."

She took a tissue that was offered and dabbed beneath her eyes so she didn't ruin her makeup.

"Okay. Let's move on," Sara suggested. "Elise, how was the honeymoon? Gorgeous and relaxing?"

Her newlywed sister beamed. "It was absolutely everything fairy tales are made of."

"You deserve that," Delilah chimed in as she took her own seat. "We all deserve happiness and I think we're all moving in the direction of the greatest times of our lives."

Sara smiled and clutched her tissue. "I agree."

She couldn't help but think of the man back at her home whom she'd shared the most erotic few days with. They'd gotten his stuff from his rental, made some serious use of that hot tub one last time, and he'd settled into her guest bedroom...the one right next to hers.

"So, should we discuss the gala?" Elise asked. "I just need to be brought up to speed on where we stand on final details."

Sara pulled herself back to reality and reached for her laptop over the stack of papers. After firing up her list, she ran down everything that still needed attention.

"We need to finalize the desserts for the caterer," she told her sisters. "The rest of the food is done."

"It's Christmas, so we have to do a red velvet cupcake or cookie or something," Elise stated. "Other than that, I don't care."

"We need a classic white," Sara added.

"Chocolate," Dee told them. "You can't have a party and not have something chocolate."

Elise shrugged. "I guess just let them know we need those three flavors and to do what they think. A variety would be great and I think finger-type desserts are best. Something easy for the waitstaff to serve either in delicate clear glasses or a cookie sort."

Sara typed in her notes and would call later today. She went over the parking and valet and the decorators' last-minute questions. Once that was all taken care of, she eased back in her seat, feeling accomplished already and they'd only been in their meeting an hour.

"Ian is coming today, right?" Elise asked.

Sara nodded. "He should be here around eleven to interview both of you."

Delilah made a little humming noise that had Sara shifting her attention. "What was that?"

Delilah shook her head. "Oh, nothing. Just didn't know if you wanted to fill Elise in on Mr. Ford."

Sara narrowed her eyes at her sister. "I was going to get to that, tattletale."

Elise stood up and walked to the door and closed it, then turned back to her sisters. "I have a feeling we're going to need privacy for this chat."

"I really was going to tell you what happened." *And is currently happening.* "There were just other things to get to first."

Elise reclaimed her chair and crossed her arms over her chest as she stared back at Sara. Her fiery red hair around her shoulders made her seem a little intimidating, but really, the woman couldn't say a word. She'd just married one of their clients after her own heated affair when they'd been locked in the castle basement.

"Ian and I have a mutual understanding—"

"You had sex," Elise finished. "I'm assuming that's what you're dancing around. So was it a one-time thing or is this ongoing?"

"One time."

"He moved in with me."

Delilah and Sara spoke at once and Sara cringed when both sisters gasped in her direction.

"Moved in with you?" Delilah questioned. "Are you out of your mind? He's not staying, Sara. You can't get tangled up in the man who is writing the most important piece our distillery has ever known."

"I know he's not staying, but it's ridiculous for him to have a rental when we're enjoying each other's company."

Why was she defending herself? She was a grown woman living her life to the fullest. Anything going on between her and Ian was their business.

"I'm only letting you guys know because I don't keep secrets," she added. "I'm not looking for permission or acceptance."

Sara leveled a stare at Delilah before she turned to Elise to do the same. Silence settled heavily among them and she absolutely hated any animosity or turmoil with the two people she treasured most in this world. But she also had to stand up for herself and do what she thought was best in her own life.

"We just worry." Elise dropped her arms and eased forward in her chair. "You all worried about me when Antonio came into my life. It's just natural."

Sara softened and sank back into her seat. "I know, I know. We love each other and that's just the way things are. But I swear, I know what I'm doing and I'm well aware Ian isn't the staying type."

"She's not very convincing," Delilah whispered in Elise's direction.

"I was in denial, too," Elise replied.

Sara's focus shifted from one sister to the other as they chattered back and forth.

Sara smacked her hands on the table. "I'm right here."

"And falling fast for a total stranger who will break your heart," Delilah scolded. "Just be careful and guard yourself. That's all we ask."

Yeah, well, she could only guard so much. She was human and formed attachments, but she was also being smart. She knew what this was and wasn't. And maybe she was enjoying herself and getting caught up in the moment, but that's how she lived her life. She wanted to take in each second and be happy instead of looking to the end and sadness.

"Regardless of how we end things, none of this will affect the piece Ian is writing on Angel's Share."

Her sisters didn't look so convinced, but Sara knew Ian would write an amazing piece and he would be honest. There was nothing not to like here and he hadn't had a bad experience. So far he'd loved the tastings and he was fascinated with the grounds and the history of an old castle nestled in the Kentucky hills. She knew he planned to talk to their rivals, but Sara wasn't worried about that, either. Competition was natural in any industry.

Sara wasn't going to keep discussing this any fur-ther. Her sisters would just have to trust her judgment and once they talked with Ian later, they could see for themselves that he was a genuine guy. He might be reserved and quiet, but he wasn't deceitful or working on some other plot. He wasn't using her because there was nothing for him to gain and he'd had no idea who she was when they first met.

There was that very realistic voice that wouldn't shut up, though. Ian would be leaving and she would have to just accept that they weren't a couple. No matter the secrets they shared or the memories they made, this moment in time would be locked here forever and nothing would ever be added.

Twelve

"The whole setup and story is so remarkable."

Ian followed Elise and Delilah into the conference room after they'd given him a mock tour. They'd wanted him to get the same experience that a customer coming through would have. It was different from the behind-the-scenes tour Sara had given him when he'd first arrived. He'd quizzed them on various aspects of their part of the business as they'd walked and talked. They'd stayed out of the way of actual tours happening, but Ian was impressed with the number of people that came through Angel's Share during any given day.

"We'd like to finish up in here." Delilah gestured for him to go in and have a seat at the long table that stretched out from the exposed stone wall. "Then we'll set you free."

Ian rolled out one of the leather chairs and waited until the ladies came in and took a seat before he relaxed. Though he felt like he was about to face a firing squad, he attempted to maintain his posture and eye contact. No way in hell was he about to look weak in front of Sara's sisters.

"I've enjoyed my time today," he admitted. "I was anxious to get to know the two of you after spending so much time with Sara. You're all quite different, but each powerful in your own department. Everything works together like one cohesive unit. Flawless, really."

"Flawless." Elise smiled and nodded. "I like that because there are certainly days that don't feel flawless. I hope when we're stressed and scrambling to cover issues that arise that our clients never notice."

"No business is perfect," he told them. "May I speak with some employees to get their perspective on such a successful operation?"

"Of course," Elise replied. "We have nothing to hide."

He wasn't quite ready to ease back in his seat and breathe a sigh of relief. With the way Elise and Delilah were glaring at him across the table, he had a feeling they were about to get into the personal side of this gathering. There was no way Sara's sisters would let this opportunity pass them by to grill him or threaten him.

Regardless of the reason he initially came to Benton Springs, that had changed drastically the moment he'd met "Jane." Now he had to deal with her loyal family and faithful watchers. She was lucky to have them and very likely knew that.

Part of him had a twinge of jealousy that she had such close-knit relationships and family. The other part of him was terrified he'd gotten tangled into such a web, because getting out would be a hell of a mess.

"I can save you the time." He had to attempt to regain control of this situation…and his life with this family. "You brought me here to quiz me or threaten me about Sara."

Elise smirked, but Delilah remained staring. Tough crowd here.

"You moved in with our sister after knowing each other for only a few days," Elise started.

Damn. Sara told them he was staying with her? Clearly they had no secrets among them, but it sounded much more permanent than the situation actually was.

"I'm staying with her through the end of next week when I leave, but she has tried to convince me to stay for the gala, so maybe just a bit longer. I'm in the guest room, we're not playing house, and anything else you want to know should come from Sara."

"She's a hopeless romantic," Delilah told him.

"She's waiting for some knight to ride up to the castle."

Ian couldn't help but laugh. "She's the last woman who would need to be rescued from anything. From what I've seen, she can definitely hold her own."

Elise leaned forward and rested her hands on the table. Why did Ian suddenly feel like he was being interviewed for a position he hadn't even applied for?

"She wants to be rescued from reality," Elise told him. "She can hold her own, but she's always had this dream of a big family and that all starts with the man of her dreams."

"She knows I'm not that man." Above all else, that had to be crystal clear. "We're adults spending time together and I'm working on this article. There's nothing more to read into this."

Sara was strong, determined, sexy and independent. There wasn't a doubt in his mind that she would hate her sisters acting like she was anything less.

Ian came to his feet. "No disrespect, ladies, but if we are done with the business portion, I'm going to head out. If there's a problem with this situation, you should take that up with your sister instead of talking to me like she's incapable of making her own decisions. You might be worried for her, but I assure you she can handle her own."

He scooted the seat back and started for the door. Before he crossed the threshold, he heard them murmur.

"I like him."

"Yeah. So do I."

And that might be the most terrifying part of his day. He wasn't trying to win these ladies over. He was here for a job, damn it. When did this project shift from business to personal and how the hell had he lost so much control?

Sara sat in her car in her driveway and stared at the number on her cell. All she had to do was hit the final button. She'd been waiting for nearly ten minutes now. There was no going back once she pressed it and this one simple call would change so many lives forever.

She'd never been so nervous in her life. Her hands shook, her stomach rolled. She was just going to have to do it before she completely lost her nerve.

Without thinking, she pressed the button and put the call through her car. She couldn't hold on to the phone right now, she had too many nerves. The first ring seemed to echo through her vehicle. She closed her eyes as the call went on to the second ring.

Maybe the voice mail would kick on and she could just hang up and call when she had more courage.

"Hello."

Her eyes flew open at the male voice that answered. But that male voice belonged to her father.

"Hi, um, Mr. Mills?"

"Yes. Who is this?"

"My name is Sara Hawthorne. You don't know

me and I'm not selling anything, so please don't hang up." She reached up and gripped the steering wheel, needing something to cling to. "I have reason to believe you are my biological father."

Silence. There was no noise coming through the speakers now, but at least he hadn't hung up.

"There was no easy way to lead into that," she quickly rambled on. "My mother was Carla Akers from Benton Springs, Kentucky."

Trenton muttered the name beneath his breath as if his past had just come out of nowhere. She couldn't imagine what was rolling through his mind right now, but she wanted to put him at ease.

"I'm sure there's no good time to just spring that news on someone," she added. "And I don't want to ruin or disrupt your life. I guess I just wanted to know if there's any chance at all that we could meet."

"I—I don't even know what to say. What was your name again?"

"Sara. Sara Hawthorne. I live in Benton Springs. I believe you used to live here for a short time, as well."

"Do you have proof? You have to understand I'm not only caught off guard, I'm skeptical."

Sara released the steering wheel and started to normalize her breathing. He was talking to her and that's all she could have asked for. She really hadn't known what to expect, but so far, she was still hopeful.

"I just recently found out who my birth mother

was," she explained. "I was raised by her sister. I hired an investigator to find you and she does have proof. Of course we could do a DNA test, but I've seen a photo of you and, well, I look just like you."

More silence. This poor man was trying to process so much in a short amount of time.

"You don't have to answer me now about meeting," she went on. "And I promise I don't want anything from you other than to know if you'd like to see me. I don't need money or anything else. I just... needed to talk to you."

"I don't know what to say. This is a lot to take in and I can't just assume."

"Of course not," she agreed, still holding on to hope. "Listen, you have my number now. If I never hear from you, I'll know you just want to move on and I understand. But if you decide you want to meet, to just see if this is real or not, I'm here. No pressure."

Again, Trenton's end was completely silent and the tension coupled with the unknown had Sara almost regretting her decision to call.

"I didn't mean to interrupt your life and I apologize if I did that." She closed her eyes once again and dropped her head back against the headrest. "I'll just... I'll let you go. Thanks for listening to me."

She disconnected the call before she could beg or demand an answer. Tears clogged her throat as the impact of the last several days caught up with her. Or maybe the emotions came because the control was out of her hands now. Whatever happened, or didn't happen, would be up to Trenton.

Sara took a minute to let the tears flow. She deserved a self-pity party, especially now that she had privacy. There was so much going on in her life. She'd taken some of the biggest leaps just in the past week between getting involved with Ian and calling her father. Never did she dream she'd be in this position where her feelings were all over the place.

But sometimes taking those big leaps had bigger rewards. So tears were fine for now, but she needed to get hold of herself and concentrate on what she could control.

Sara wiped her tears and pulled in a deep breath. She couldn't help but wonder how long she should wait for a call or if she should just come to the realization that maybe her father didn't want to upend the family life he'd built. Regardless, she was proud of herself for reaching out and stating her case.

As she stepped from her car and headed toward the house, she realized Ian wasn't here. She'd left the distillery nearly an hour ago and he'd been gone long before that. She hadn't talked to him since his interviews with her sisters and all they said was things went well.

Something must have happened for them to have been tight-lipped.

No matter, Sara still wondered where Ian had gone to. He certainly didn't owe her any explanations or need to check in, but she was curious. There was really no protocol for this temporary living arrangement so all she could do was go about her evening and not focus on all the balls she had up in the air.

Thirteen

The moment Ian walked in the front door, some delicious aroma hit him. Something warm and yeasty…a scent that definitely reminded him of his childhood. Instant memories flooded him of his mother in the kitchen or him hanging out in the back of her bakery. She always loved trying new recipes and he was her favorite taste-tester.

He couldn't help but smile and Ian wondered when the last time he smiled about that memory was. Usually when he thought of his mother, an onslaught of guilty emotions threatened to consume him. But for now, there was a sense of peace.

He must be sleep-deprived, because how the hell

else could he explain that a damn smell made him happy? That was absurd.

Or maybe that was just another way Sara had infiltrated his world. He hadn't even given her his entire backstory, yet she was slowly healing his shattered heart.

Ian carried his bag to the back of the house toward the kitchen. His stomach growled as he headed past the steps and down the hall. Music and some off-key singing also greeted him. The minute he crossed over the threshold, he stilled.

Sara stood with her back to him just swaying to the classic tunes as she attempted to sing with Ol' Blue Eyes. She stirred something in a pot without a care in the world except her duet with Frank. Ian leaned against the doorjamb and watched those swaying hips. Never in his life did he think he'd want to come home to a woman in his space, but he couldn't lie that...

No. He shouldn't be getting swept up in this moment. This wasn't his home and Sara wasn't his woman. Falling into some familial fantasy was ridiculous.

Sara tapped her spoon on the edge of the pan and spun around—her singing immediately coming to an abrupt halt.

"Oh, sorry. I didn't hear the door alarm over the music." She shut the melody off and turned back to face him, pasting on a wide smile. "I didn't know if you'd be hungry when you came in, so I just made some cheesy potato soup and sourdough bread. Nothing fancy, but I like comfort foods when it's cold outside."

Sara reached for the towel hanging on her oven door and wiped her hands. Then she brushed her hair away from her face and rushed to grab some bowls from the cabinet.

"You don't have to eat, but it's here if you're hungry. I'm not sure what all you got into today, so…"

Ian stepped farther into the kitchen and placed his bag on one of the stools at the island. Sara started muttering something else and trying to get dinner set up, but her hands shook and she looked like she was on the verge of tears.

What the hell had happened today?

He stepped in behind her and wrapped his arms around her waist, pulling her back against his chest.

"Relax," he murmured. "You don't need to do anything extra for me, especially when you've had a hell of a day."

Her body went lax against his as she sat the bowl on the counter.

"I don't know what happened," he went on, "but I've got you."

He didn't know where these reassuring words were coming from, but she clearly needed them… and maybe he needed this, too. His emotions since walking through the door had been up and down, but Sara had some inner turmoil that was causing her to panic.

"How do you even know how my day was?" she asked.

"Because you're on edge and can't stand still."

Sara turned and wrapped her arms around his neck. Her lips grazed his skin as her warm breath tickled the side of his face. Something seemed to just click into place, but he had no clue what because he hadn't been looking for anything to "click." Maybe he was just feeling that sense of pride for being in the right place at the right time. Clearly Sara needed someone right now and he wasn't sorry he was that guy.

"I have a bad feeling I'm about to dump my entire life story on you," she sniffed against the side of his neck.

"Was that a warning for me to run?" he asked.

"This is your only chance to save yourself."

Ian tightened his hold. "I'm not worried about me. Let's hear it."

A moment later, Sara broke down. He hadn't expected tears before the story, but there was obvious pain she was working through.

Ian reached behind her and turned off the burner, then bent down and lifted her. With one arm behind her back and one beneath her knees, he carried her to the adjoining living area and sank down onto the couch. He cradled her against him and attempted to soothe her with soft strokes up and down her back. The way she trembled against him had his heart clenching and he wished like hell he could do something to fix this, but he wasn't quite clear what "this" was.

The glow from the Christmas tree and the flames in the fireplace kept the room in soft lighting. He couldn't see her face, but he slid her stray strands over her shoulder and let her take this moment. Everyone had a breaking point, even him. He just always kept himself in check unless he was alone. And even at that, he hadn't had a private moment in years. He couldn't allow himself to go to that dark place in his mind because he truly feared he'd never recover if he accepted the fact that he was responsible for his mother's death.

Oh, the doctors and social workers told him the accident wasn't his fault, but if he hadn't been arguing with his mother and had her distracted on that snowy road, perhaps she'd still be alive.

Sara sniffed once again and eased up. Her damp eyes met his and that helpless feeling rolling through him was most certainly unwelcome. She trusted him with her emotions or she wouldn't be so vulnerable and open. Which made this moment even more amazing. She was brave enough to trust him with her fears and there was no place else he'd rather be than right here, right now.

"I really didn't mean to just cut loose like that."

Ian shrugged. "It's better than your singing."

Sara swatted his chest and laughed…which was the exact response he'd been hoping for. She needed to have just a little of that pressure removed from her shoulders and that was the only way he knew to do it.

"I wasn't expecting an audience," she informed him as she swiped the moisture from her cheeks.

When she started to scramble off his lap, Ian tightened his hold around her waist. "Talk to me."

She pulled in a deep breath and shook her head. "It's just all caught up with me and you found me at a weak moment. I'm sure you know nothing about being weak."

"You're not weak, you're human, and we're not talking about me right now."

"You never want to talk about you," she countered. "That's how I know you're not weak. I have a roller coaster of a day, hell a week, and I lose it."

"You're entitled to lose it. Did something happen with your sisters? Did they tell you about my visit?"

Sara's eyes narrowed. "They didn't say anything, which makes me nervous. What happened?"

No way in hell was Ian going to get into that little conversation he'd had with Elise and Delilah. That was between Sara and them.

"We had a good interview," he replied. "So if the issue isn't them, what is it? Does it have anything to do with that phone call of yours the other day?"

Sara nodded. "You know my sisters and I are all adopted? Well, what we found out a few months ago is that our adoptive mother, Milly, was actually our aunt. Her sister was our biological mom."

"That must have been quite a surprise."

"That wasn't even the most shocking part," Sara went on. "We found out our mom had been in and out of rehabs, had given birth to the three of us and, I'm sure I don't need to tell you, we all have different fathers."

Ian smiled. "That's apparent, but you all are very strong women, so you must have gotten that from your mother's side of the family."

"We definitely got our strong will from Milly. She raised us to be who we are today, but she never told us the truth. We can only assume to spare us the pain of knowing who our mother was or the mistakes she'd made."

Ian could see that being a very strong possibility. He ran his hand up and down her thigh, silently urging her to keep going.

"Elise never wanted to know who her biological father was and Delilah got the information on hers, but never reached out." Sara swiped at her eyes once more and then started drawing a pattern on the back of his hand. "I hired an investigator and that's who called the other day with the contact info for my father. As you saw I was a bit overwhelmed on my office floor and maybe even more so today."

Ian waited for her to keep going. At least she'd stopped crying and she wasn't shaking. Her fingertip continued a circular pattern and she seemed mesmerized as she continued speaking.

"I called Trenton Mills today," she murmured. "He's a teacher in Knoxville with a wife and a son.

He's got a family and when I called him, he was so taken off guard, I think I ruined his life."

Ian turned his hand over and laced his fingers with hers. "You didn't ruin his life," he told her. "Look at me."

Her tear-filled eyes came up to his and he raised his brows to drive his point home.

"You didn't," he repeated. "The man is going to be shocked and maybe not so welcoming right off the bat. If he held a conversation with you, then that's a good sign. How did you leave things with him before you hung up?"

"I said if he wanted to meet, he could call me. Basically I gave him an out and said that if he didn't want anything to do with me, I would understand if I didn't hear from him."

Ian pulled her against his chest and held tight. "That's all you can do. Give him time to process everything. Who knows, it's Christmas so maybe he'll call and you'll get the greatest gift."

"I've already thought of that. I couldn't ask for more than just one more talk with him. Even if he calls, I just liked hearing his voice." A soft laugh escaped her. "That probably sounds crazy."

"Not at all. I never knew my father, either, so I get it."

Sara trailed her hand up over his shoulder, her fingertips brushed along his jawline as she spoke. "Did you ever look for him?"

"No. After my mother passed, I pretty much remained in foster care for the next six months and then I took what little savings my mom had and money from the sale of her bakery and I moved south. I wanted as far away as possible."

Away from the memories, away from the nightmares that had plagued him for months. It had taken a total reset once he'd gotten to Miami. He'd promised himself the minute he stepped foot into the town that his new life would not involve emotions or attachments. The closest thing he had to a relationship was Nigel.

"And you've been pushing people away since."

Sara's words penetrated the moment and pierced that wall he'd put up around his heart. He never spoke about his past, ever. Yet with Sara, he found himself actually wanting to.

What the hell was happening here?

"Maybe I have," he admitted. "Life has been easier that way."

Sara pressed her palm to his chest and lifted her head. "That's the saddest thing I've ever heard."

"Do I look sad?"

She stared at him for a moment, then ran the tip of her finger between his brows. "You do."

Well, damn. He hadn't expected her to say that. He'd worked so hard on being strong, resilient, maybe even stony. But he'd never wanted to come across as sad because if anyone saw that, they would offer pity and that's the last thing he ever wanted from anyone.

"I'm sad because I'm hungry," he countered, needing to get the focus off of his backstory. "What do you say we eat?"

She offered a slight smile. "I'll get the table set."

"No." That was another level of intimacy he couldn't enter into, not even with her. "Let's eat in here and watch a movie."

Sara quirked a brow, but ultimately nodded. "Deal. Get the movie set up and I'll get everything else."

He thought he'd get some pushback on that one, but thankfully he didn't. Maybe a casual dinner and movie would help soothe both of their souls tonight.

Fourteen

"That was the worst movie I've ever seen." Sara moved her feet from Ian's lap and stood to stretch. "I should have never let you choose."

"But you did and you're a better person for watching. There's nothing like old Westerns."

Sara snorted. "You got that right. I thought we'd watch something old like a nice black-and-white with Ingrid Bergman or Rita Hayworth."

"You didn't put a request in." Ian rose to his full height and stared down at her. "But you did make a hell of a dinner."

"Soup and bread? You really need higher expectations."

He took a step closer and rested his hands on her

shoulders. "I've found my expectations are changing, perhaps better than they've ever been."

Those talented fingers started kneading her knots and Sara couldn't help the groan that escaped her.

"If your nonfiction book doesn't work out you could make some serious money being a masseur."

He was constantly rubbing on her: feet, thighs, shoulders. She wasn't about to complain, either. The man had magic hands...in the bedroom and out. Not that they'd made it to her bedroom, he still put the brakes on that.

"Do you have an early day tomorrow?" he asked.

"Not really. The busiest part of the distillery right now is rush orders for the holidays. I'm working on planning the governor's daughter's wedding for the spring and getting the rest of the venue options locked in for other weddings. Elise's day has blown up our social media even though she just had an intimate ceremony."

Ian threaded his fingers through her hair and tipped her head back. "We're supposed to get more snow tonight and I didn't like the idea of you out too early."

Sara grinned and slid her arms around his waist. "And here I thought you just wanted to keep me in your bed."

"That, too," he confirmed.

He dipped his head and grazed his lips over hers. Sara closed her eyes and let him lead the moment. Maybe she could take half a day off tomorrow. There was nothing she couldn't work on from home and she'd already finalized the last-minute Christmas at the Castle details. All there was to do now was…Ian.

She reached for the button on his dress shirt and wondered if the man owned any casual clothes. He'd shed the vest, though, so now all she had to do was get him out of this shirt and his pants.

She, on the other hand, had changed immediately when she'd gotten home and Ian probably wondered why she looked homeless in her own house. But her favorite cozy sweats and off the shoulder sweater were perfect for a wintery night in.

The only light they had now was the fireplace and the crisp white lights from her Christmas tree. And once she peeled that shirt off of him, she wondered why she hadn't thought to capture that chiseled body more in this glowing effect.

"You look at me like…"

"What?" she asked, glancing up. "Like I want to devour you? That's because I do."

"That will have to wait because I'm taking my time with you tonight."

Oh, that sounded like the most delicious warning and promise all rolled into one.

Sara took a step back and quickly removed her clothes, leaving her standing in only a white cami and matching boy shorts.

Ian's eyes traveled over her like he was taking in the sight for the very first time. But in all honesty, they had always been rushed and frantic and eager to pleasure each other. Tonight was different. Tonight *felt* different.

That vise around her heart tightened and Sara knew she was going to be in trouble, but she couldn't stop how she felt any more than she could stop wanting this man. So she might as well just go with it and worry about the ramifications later.

"How do you make everything look so damn sexy?" he murmured, reaching for her.

"I'm just me," she said, shrugging, not really knowing how to answer that.

"Yeah." He pulled her close and tipped her head back to grip her chin. "That's what makes you so damn irresistible."

Sara let him take over, let him do whatever he wanted, because she wanted to forget. She wanted to erase the fear that stemmed from the phone call with her father, and she needed to eradicate the sickening feeling that Ian would be out of her life much too soon…because she wanted to hold on to him forever.

Ian had just sat down at Sara's kitchen island with his laptop and his first cup of coffee for the morning when his cell rang. Nigel's name came up on the screen and Ian popped in his earphones, then tapped the speaker so he could have his hands free.

"Morning," he greeted. "What's up?"

"Just checking in," Nigel claimed. "I hadn't heard from you in a few days. You ready to move back north or will you be returning?"

Ian chuckled. "I'm ready to hang up this coat and get back to the sunshine and heat."

"Glad to hear it. I mean, you're moving on no matter what, but I like knowing you're not leaving me completely." Nigel let out a sigh and continued. "Seriously, though, how does everything look? Are you on track for the first-of-the-year deadline?"

"I am. I've been compiling notes and writing the piece as I go."

After his interesting interaction with Elise and Delilah yesterday, he'd spent the rest of the day at Rise and Grind. He'd ultimately tried the scones and his past and present collided. He could see a bridge between the two and he had Sara to thank for something so trivial, yet meaningful. He'd also found the perfect quiet corner to get some much-needed work done.

"I'm likely staying for the Christmas at the Castle gala at the distillery, but I should be back just before Christmas."

"So you'll be here for dinner at my house? Because Beth is making your favorite trifle dessert."

Ian had spent every Christmas with Nigel since he'd come to Miami. Where else would he be?

"Tell her I wouldn't miss it. And this piece on Angel's Share might actually come in early."

"In a hurry to be done here at *Elite*?" Nigel joked. "You've never had a project early in your entire career."

"This one is different," Ian admitted, toying with

the handle on his coffee mug. Of course the em-
bossed front was the distillery logo. "This place is
fascinating."

"And the women?"

"Also fascinating."

"So fascinating you canceled the rental?" Nigel
asked.

Sara swept into the kitchen and padded straight
to the coffeepot. She'd just gotten out of the shower
and that familiar floral aroma left a trail behind her.
She sat her mug down to fill and shot him a naughty
grin over her shoulder.

Apparently all of last night and this morning had
put her in a good mood. He was in a pretty good
place in his life, as well.

"How did you find that out?" Ian asked, refocusing on Nigel's question.

"Considering the magazine was paying for your
travels, the invoice and cancellation were brought
to my attention from accounting."

All the more reason he needed to get away from
a regular job. He could do what he wanted, when
he wanted. Not that Nigel cared, but Ian didn't care
for being questioned on his actions.

"I found something better."

Sara went to the fridge and bent over, looking
for her creamer. The little T-shirt she'd thrown on
moved up her thighs and Ian merely sat back and ad-
mired the view. Even with her silly, fluffy pink slip-
pers, she looked so adorable and too damn perfect.

All of this was starting to feel too perfect…but it couldn't be. This wasn't what he came here for and he had other aspirations. Settling down in one place, with hellish weather, was not his idea of a good time. It all sounded like a trap.

"And does she know you're not the staying kind?" Nigel asked.

"Yeah. That's been discussed."

Nigel let out a grunt, of acknowledgment or disapproval, Ian wasn't certain. No matter what his friend and boss thought, Ian didn't do bonds or commitments or anything else that was outside of furthering his career. Granted, his career as a journalist had taken off years ago and he was at the top of his game now, but he was so set in his ways and just fine with the life he'd created.

"You sound different."

Nigel's statement interjected right through Ian's thoughts.

"Different? How?"

"I can't put my finger on it. You almost sound… happy."

Ian ground his teeth as he stared across the kitchen to Sara as she poured the perfect amount of creamer.

"Why do people keep thinking I'm not happy?" he demanded.

Sara tossed another look over her shoulder and merely shrugged with a smile.

"Because you've always been like a robot just going through daily motions," Nigel explained.

"Living your life and simply being alive are completely different things."

Sara stirred her coffee and blew before taking that first sip. When she closed her eyes and sipped again, Nigel's words somehow made perfect sense. Sara lived her life. She enjoyed each and every aspect including something as mundane as morning brew.

"Everyone is different," Ian replied.

No way was he getting into anything too deep this early in the day and especially with Sara standing within earshot. Nigel had a wife, children and an incredibly successful company. Ian was thrilled for the man, but that didn't mean that lifestyle was meant for Ian.

"I'll be back after the gala," Ian informed him. "Don't worry about this project. I've got everything covered."

"It's not the project I'm worried about."

Ian disconnected the call and reached for his mug. He was a big boy and, while he appreciated the love and respect from Nigel, Ian didn't need life or love advice.

Love. What a ridiculous term to even try to fit into his life. He wouldn't even understand how to love a woman, not the way one deserved. And Sara absolutely deserved the best. Maybe if he'd met her when he'd been younger and he hadn't created such a jaded world for himself...but there was no sense in even allowing his thoughts to travel down that path. He was passing through and considered himself damn lucky to have met someone like Sara Hawthorne.

"Are you staying here all day?"

Sara stood on the other side of the island, cupping her mug with both hands and staring at him, waiting for him to come back to reality.

"If it's snowing, I'm not moving from this spot."

Sara rolled her eyes. "You really have a problem with this and I'm going to break you of it."

Ian shook his head. "Doubtful. There's a reason I've lived in Miami most of my life."

"Yeah, fear," she countered. "But since you don't want to discuss your past, which I respect, I have to deal with the Ian I know now and I'm here to help you."

What was it with her and Nigel wanting to help him all of a sudden? What part of his actions or his life did they see that they deemed necessary to "fix"?

"Why don't you go on to work and I'll stay here and get some things done on my end?" he suggested.

Sara's smile spread across her face, but instead of looking wholesome and adorable like always, she seemed almost…maniacal.

"You can stay here," she agreed. "But I need to run out and I'll be right back."

She dashed from the kitchen and Ian instantly had a pit in his stomach. Whatever she had planned, he had a feeling he was not going to like this.

Fifteen

"You've got to be kidding me."

Sara clapped her gloved hands and laughed at Ian's face. The poor man looked like he was getting ready for a root canal without the Novocain. But she wanted to tackle whatever demons he had, and since she didn't really know what he was dealing with, this was all she could think of.

"Come on. Like you never went sleigh riding as a kid?" she asked.

Ian nodded. "Of course I did, when I was little and not afraid to break a bone."

"Don't be so dramatic," she scolded. "You're not going to break a bone."

"Maybe not, but splitting these snow pants is a real possibility," he growled.

"Yeah, well, Camden is just a little shorter than you and that's the only place I could think of to get you snow gear spur-of-the-moment."

Delilah had thought Sara was an absolute fool for taking the day off and playing in the snow with Ian. But thankfully Sara wasn't asking for opinions and only wanted to borrow Cam's clothes.

"I'm worried about my nether regions," Ian added.

"I'm here to make sure you have fun and I'll watch out for those regions," she joked. "Neither of us wants harm to come to that territory."

Ian turned and looked at the slope going down her backyard, then shifted back to her.

"How about a snowball fight instead?" he suggested. "It's damn cold out here and that sounds quicker, and less stress on the seam of these pants."

"Snowball fight is after the sleigh ride." She picked up the two-person sled and settled it into the snow. "Hop on and then I'll get in between your legs."

He eyed her another minute like he was about to argue, but she just pointed to the sleigh.

"How the hell did I lose control?" he muttered as he awkwardly sank and fell into the sled.

Snow crunched and gave way beneath her boots as she made her way to her spot. After settling in, she grabbed the rope in front.

"Ready?" she called.

"No."

Too bad. She rocked her body and pushed off the snow with one hand while steering the sled with the other. Ian's arms banded around her waist as the crisp snow rushed up to her face. Thankfully she had her scarf wrapped around her and her hat pulled low. The rush of the slide had Sara squealing, but she had a feeling Ian sat behind her with his eyes closed.

She tugged on the rope to the side, hoping to go just a bit farther down the slope, but her plan went askew. The sled tipped, sending her and Ian into the snow on their sides.

Laughing, Sara pushed her way up to her knees and glanced to Ian, who was still lying in the snow. He'd rolled to his back and stared up at the sky.

"Nobody would believe this if they could see me," he muttered. "Not one person."

"What? That you're having fun?"

"Is that what this is called?"

Sara gathered up snow in her glove and packed it tight before launching the ball at his chest. Ian wasted no time in forming his own and tossing them right back. But he had a faster process than she did and all she could do was laugh and use the sled as a shield.

"I'm waving the white flag," she yelled. "You win."

"Does that mean we're going back inside?"

She peered around the sled. "You don't want to

do the hill again? Just one more time? You can take the lead."

The snowball in his hand dropped in front of him as he stared back at her. She'd never seen him in any element other than professional, but he looked good here. Too good. He'd slid fluidly into her world and she'd watched every step of the way, disregarding any warning bells that had gone off in her head.

She'd made a grave mistake and fallen for Ian Ford.

Why the hell had she ever thought she could compartmentalize her emotions? She threw every part of herself into every aspect of her life. Having a one-night stand had never been her norm for good reason…because she formed bonds so easily.

And if they'd just shared that one night, maybe she could have gotten him out of her head, but there had been many nights and days and now here she was with her heart on the line.

"Will that make you happy?" he asked. "Just one more time?"

She could do this all day with him and lock each second in her memory bank.

"One more time," she agreed. "Then we'll go inside and get warm by the fire."

"You need a hot tub."

"I'm realizing that more and more."

Sara used the sled as leverage to come to her feet. She slipped a little before regaining her footing, then pointed toward the top of the incline.

"This is the only downside to sledding," she told him. "Climbing back up."

"It's the chafing for me."

Sara snorted as she started to climb. "You'll be just fine and back in your work clothes in no time."

She should have grabbed some sweats from Cam as well, but those likely would have been ill-fitting, too. She couldn't reprogram Ian into the man she wanted him to be or the man she thought he could be. She adored who he was, but she wished she could figure out what had made him into such a cautious, wary man who was too straitlaced for his own good.

And he was leaving next week. She'd heard him talking on the phone earlier, and even though she'd known it was coming, that didn't make the fact any less depressing.

All she knew was he was staying through the gala and then he'd be gone. There was no chance of him changing his mind and she wasn't naive enough to believe that a heated fling would make someone uproot their life and start over. This wasn't her fairy tale at all…this was just an amazing moment in time that she'd have to remember forever.

Ian Ford had definitely marked a spot on her heart that could only be reserved for him, and that was okay. She just had a sinking feeling she'd compare every man that came into her life to Ian from here on out and there wasn't a doubt in her mind, there was no comparison.

* * *

"You have to get the red," Elise declared.

Sara turned side to side in the mirror and really did love the look of this gold gown, but red was her color and that other one she'd just taken off really did accentuate her figure.

"Agree," Delilah chimed in, stepping up beside Sara on the platform.

Queen was their go-to boutique when they needed upscale dresses. Where else could they shop in private and have champagne served to them?

"Wow." Sara took in Delilah in the white shimmering gown with a high neck and long sleeves. "You look like an angel."

"I have a bad feeling if I wear white, I'll spill red wine all over me, but I do love this one."

Elise came to stand near the platform. The sisters all surveyed one another in the mirror and Sara was so thrilled that they were able to do this, that they'd come this far. Hopes and dreams were continually being made each day they were successful in their business.

"You have to get it," Elise insisted. "Nobody could look that good in that dress except you."

Delilah gave a half turn and looked at the back of the dress, which was scooped low with more shimmer detail. Sara glanced to Elise and took in the black strapless gown with gold beading around the bust.

"That's gorgeous, too," Sara told her sister.

"We're all looking pretty damn good. Let me put the red dress back on and let's see how we'll all look as a team."

Sara stepped off the platform and rushed back to her dressing room. Her cell vibrated on the chaise and she paused to check the text from Ian.

Let me know before you come home. I have a surprise and it's not ready.

A surprise? Well, that was unexpected, and she loved surprises. Smiling, she hit Reply.

Can't wait!

So many thoughts ran through her mind as she wrestled out of this gown and into the other. She literally had no clue what he could possibly be doing or have bought her. Was this for an early Christmas? They weren't doing gifts...were they? Maybe she should have gotten him something, too.

Damn it. Now she was confused.

She had no idea what to get him and the only thing she wanted this year was to hear from her father. It had been days since she called and she didn't know how much longer she should give him before she just gave up and moved on.

Sara eased open the door and stepped out of her dressing room just as the associate came in with a tray of champagne and a silver bowl of strawberries.

"Ladies, you all look amazing." She sat the tray down on the white table and offered a wide smile. "Can I grab some accessories and shoe options for each of you?"

"Absolutely." Delilah beamed. "I think these are the dresses we're going with, so bring us whatever you think."

"Give me just a few minutes."

The experienced associate left them alone, and that was the perk of always working with the same woman. She knew their likes and dislikes as well as their sizes. She knew when to help and when to give them privacy. Sara appreciated a smart businesswoman.

"That red is hands down the best one for you," Elise told Sara as she caught her reflection in the mirror. "I'm so excited for this Christmas party, you guys. I want the castle to not only be known for great bourbon, but our amazing events."

They'd set long-term goals and were knocking them off one at a time. Their projected plans were all falling beautifully into place and Sara couldn't believe this was her life, that she actually got to have a dream career with her very best friends.

She hadn't told them about reaching out to her father yet, but she really wanted to share that with them. They could offer her that boost of support because she was desperately wishing he'd text or call…anything at all.

"I have some news to share with you guys." Sara

went for a glass of champagne and grabbed one to hold her hands steady. "I called my father and spoke with him."

"What?"

"Are you serious?"

Her sisters spoke at the same time, both of them staring at her with wide eyes and open mouths.

Sara nodded. "Yeah, um, he was shocked, obviously. He didn't hang up on me and listened to what I had to say, so that's something. But he didn't agree to meet with me or anything. I gave him an out and just asked him to think about it and call me if he wanted to know more or meet up."

Delilah reached for her own champagne glass. "How long ago was that?"

"A few days now. I didn't want to say anything yet because I was hoping he'd call or text and then I could tell you guys that. But I couldn't hold it in anymore. I'm so anxious with every sound my phone makes that it's going to be him, but nothing so far."

"Okay, well, you took a big step." Delilah sipped on her champagne and grabbed a glass, passing it to Elise. "I won't promise that he will call, but I would think once he starts thinking about this more and more, he'll want to know you. I wouldn't dismiss this so quickly or worry quite yet."

"Agreed," Elise stated, stepping off the platform. "I assume he'll call, but we don't know this man, so there's no way to gauge his reaction. We're going to all be optimistic. It's Christmas, right? If there's ever a time for miracles and renewal, now is it."

Sara took a drink and hoped her sisters were right. Just hearing them assure her eased some of her nerves. Talking to Ian had helped, too. She hadn't expected him to be such a great listener. She just wished like hell he'd open up to her as well. Was he going to leave town and keep that area of his past a secret? Did anyone know what he'd been through? Obviously his social workers, but did he ever have a counselor or someone he trusted wholeheartedly to help him through those difficult days?

Delilah sat her champagne flute down and glanced back to Elise.

"Don't you want your champagne?" she asked.

Elise glanced from Delilah to Sara. "Yeah, I do. I mean, I love champagne, but…"

Elise burst into tears. "I'm pregnant."

Sara was glad she'd sat her glass down. Pregnant?

"Oh, honey, this is great news." Sara stepped forward and wrapped her arms around her sister. "Our first baby of the family. This is exciting. Is Antonio happy?"

Elise sniffed. "He's already choosing names and paint colors for the nursery and I just found out yesterday."

Sara eased back as Delilah came in for a hug, too.

"You're still in shock, but I'm so excited," Dee

stated. "You guys are going to be the best parents and I'm going to be an aunt. I better start shopping."

Sara laughed, already knowing her own credit card was about to take a big hit. But she didn't care. Elise and Antonio were just starting their married lives together and building their family. The next generation was on the way and Sara couldn't be happier or more excited.

The associate stepped back in with boxes of shoes and a variety of jewelry on a tray.

"Oh, is everything all right?" she asked, obviously seeing the tears and hugs.

"We're fine," Sara assured her. "Happy tears."

"Oh, great. Do you need me to help further or should I leave these and give you privacy?"

Delilah stepped back from Elise and offered the associate a smile. "We're good for now, but thank you so much."

Once they were alone again, Delilah cringed. "One of us is always crying when we come here."

"Yeah, last time it was you," Elise teased as she patted her damp cheeks.

Delilah had a minor crying spell when they'd been in to choose dresses for their bourbon launch. In her defense, she and Cam were on the brink of a divorce and she was absolutely heartbroken. Now they were back together and happier than ever... with their new pup, Milly.

"I'm sorry." Elise glanced to Sara and tipped her head. "I didn't mean to dampen your news about your dad. I didn't know when to tell you and I would have just done it later, but Dee handed me champagne and—"

"Do not apologize for being happy," Sara scolded. "We're all going to have ups and downs and I'm not even sure where my news falls on the spectrum."

"This is an exciting time for all of us." Delilah picked up Elise's flute and started sipping. "We're all in another chapter of our lives, but we're doing it together and that's all that matters."

Sara nodded in agreement. "True. I don't know what I'd do without you guys."

"Does that mean you want to talk about Ian and what's going on back at your house?"

Sara stilled and wished she'd taken that extra glass of champagne. Instead, she reached for a strawberry and popped one in her mouth.

"She's not going to answer that," Elise replied. "Which means she's already in too far."

"No way. Love already?" Delilah shook her head. "They haven't known each other very long."

Elise shrugged. "Who am I to judge? I married a man I was trapped in a cellar with."

Sara sighed and stepped up onto the platform to admire the dress she was going to purchase. "I'm not in love," she insisted.

Maybe heavy, heavy like and about a breath away from falling in love, but she wasn't there…yet.

"We're just having fun while he's in town. He's attending the gala and then he'll be on his way. Our

write-up in *Elite* will be glowing and amazing and
we'll pull in even more business. There's nothing
negative about our situation, whether it be personal
or professional."

The skeptical looks from her sisters in the mirror
only had Sara smiling in return. "Now, let's look
at all of these accessories and get more champagne
and some sparkling water in here."

Sixteen

This whole idea was preposterous. What was he thinking? He'd never done anything like this before, but he'd woken up and Sara had bustled around to head out the door to meet her sisters for a girls' day and her house had been so quiet.

He hadn't liked the silence. When he'd walked from his guest room just down to the kitchen to work, he'd felt…lonely. That was an emotion he hadn't felt in so long, it was almost foreign.

But he was leaving soon, so he'd have to get used to that solitary lifestyle once again.

Who knew spending almost two weeks in Kentucky with a bubbly woman who was the polar opposite of him would have his entire life turned upside down? How the hell had she managed to re-program everything he thought he knew or wanted?

He was just getting sidetracked, that's all. He was so far out of his comfort zone with everything here, his mind was just confused.

But he couldn't deny he was a little anxious for her to get home and see the surprise. He honestly couldn't believe he'd done something so extravagant for anyone, let alone the woman he'd been sleeping with for such a short time. She deserved someone to spoil her, though. He just wished like hell he didn't feel so awkward about this.

Sara was always busy making sure others were comfortable or consoled and he knew she was going through a difficult time with the worry of her father up in the air. While his surprise might make him feel uncomfortable because he'd never done something like this, he figured it would put a smile on her face. He hoped.

When the driveway alarm chimed, Ian saved his work on his laptop and closed it up. He shoved back from the kitchen island where he'd set up a make-shift office area and wondered if he should take her straight to the gift or let her unwind first.

Maybe a glass of wine? She liked wine.

Or should he pour her a bourbon?

Why was he so nervous? This wasn't his girl-friend or his wife about to walk through that door. Knowing Sara, she'd love the gesture and it would make her think of him long after he was gone.

An instant image of another man here with her churned his stomach and pissed him off, actually, but he couldn't have it both ways.

The chime from the door between the garage and the utility room echoed through to the kitchen. Moments later she stepped through and had already shed her coat and bag. She brushed her hair back away from her face and met his eyes across the room.

"Hey," she greeted with that wide smile he'd come to expect whenever she looked at him. "You gave me absolutely no hints to this surprise and it's been bugging me all day. So let me have it."

She held out her hands and danced on her toes like a giddy child and Ian couldn't help but shake his head and laugh. This woman could make any mood lift when she was around. How could anyone be upset or sad when Sara stepped into the room? She demanded happiness and stability in her part of the world. And she deserved everything she could ever want.

"I can't exactly put it in your hands," he informed her. "It's a little larger than that."

Her arms fell to her sides and her brows rose. "Did you get me a dog?"

"No animal at all."

Sara's lips pursed as she scanned the kitchen and then looked over his shoulder toward the living area. Her eyes came back to his.

"You didn't go buy new clothes because you're still wearing your dressy stuff that looks entirely too uncomfortable for a night in."

"No, I didn't buy new clothes. I don't need them."

"That's still up for debate," she stated. "So, where is this gift?"

He opened his mouth, but she held up her hands.

"Wait," she commanded. "I didn't get you any-thing for Christmas. I didn't think that's where we were at here, but if this is a Christmas present, I'm going to feel terrible."

"I didn't do this for Christmas." He closed the distance between them and took her hands in his. "I did this because I thought you'd like it and you need someone to pamper you."

Those wide, expressive eyes held his. "And is that what you're doing? Pampering me?"

"For as long as I can."

He leaned in and kissed the tip of her nose. "Fol-low me," he told her, taking her hand and leading her toward the back of the house.

"We're going outside? It's freezing."

"It is," he agreed, still leading the way.

"We're not dressed for sleigh riding and it's dark now."

"You're stating all the obvious." Ian stopped and turned to face her. "You must be nervous."

She chewed on the bottom of her lip. "Intrigued, definitely. But you don't make me nervous."

He reached out and cupped the side of her face, loving when she leaned into his touch. She shouldn't affect him so damn much, but he could look at her and be with her for—

No. Not forever. That thought was absurd and naive. She was remarkable, yes, but he was not the man for her.

"Close your eyes and let me lead you."

After the briefest of hesitations, she closed her eyes and Ian took both of her hands and carefully walked backward. When he reached the double doors, he reached out and flicked the lock open and pushed them both wide. The blast of cold air hit them, but Ian didn't care. Now that he took in the entire space he'd had done for her, he knew he'd made the right decision.

"How much farther? And are you really just going to blast me with snowballs?" she asked.

"I promise, no snow is involved with this surprise."

"Can I open my eyes yet?"

Ian angled Sara just the right way before he released her hands and stepped aside.

"Now."

He kept his focus on Sara, wanting to take in every bit of her reaction…and she didn't disappoint. Between the gasp and her hands flying up to her mouth in shock, he could finally breathe a sigh of relief that he hadn't overstepped his bounds here.

"Ian," she exclaimed. "What have you done? Oh, my word."

"I hope you like it."

She took a step toward the new hot tub that had the jets bubbling and the colored lights illuminating the water. Then she glanced around to the clear bulbs he had draped from the ceiling of the back porch and the steps leading up to the hot tub. On either side of the steps were box pillars that held fat black lanterns for an added glow.

"You did all of this today?" she asked, spinning back around toward him. "I wasn't gone that long, was I?"

"I actually made a couple of calls yesterday and had my plan put into action as soon as you were gone today." He crossed over to her where she stood on the outdoor rug beneath the hot tub steps. "And you were gone about eight hours. Plenty of time to give you a little oasis."

With all the various lighting surrounding them, plus the full moon, Sara's eyes sparkled as she stared back at him.

"I can't believe this," she murmured. "I mean, this was a lot of work. When you said surprise, I thought maybe you got me a pair of earrings or a sweater. Hell, maybe a snow sled. I never, ever expected anything like this."

Ian rested his hands on her shoulders and leaned in a little closer. "Do I strike you as the type of guy who would pick out jewelry or clothes?"

"Honestly, you don't strike me as the guy who would pull out a surprise like this, but I love it." She framed his face with her delicate hands and pressed a kiss to his lips. "I have no idea how you did this in such a short time, but I've never been more surprised or excited."

Tears welled up in her eyes and she blinked them away.

"I don't know the last time anyone surprised me with something," she admitted. "I mean, I had a surprise Sweet Sixteen party, but as far as a surprise for no reason at all… I don't even know what to say. 'Thank you' seems so small in comparison."

All along he'd thought they were different in so many ways, but he could relate. Surprises weren't something that happened to him, either, and he'd never had anyone he wanted to surprise with something. Being on the giving end was pretty amazing and seeing just how happy she was made the time and the money and the phone calls all worth it. He'd definitely paid a hefty sum to get this done on the spur of the moment, but none of that mattered. He'd pay triple to see her this happy and genuinely surprised.

Genuine. That was the perfect word that summed up Sara. She loved her life, expected nothing in return but loyalty, and gave every bit of herself to those she loved.

She blinked again and a lone tear slid down her cheek and she nestled deeper into his embrace.

"It's cold out here." She laughed. "Maybe we should make use of this hot tub."

He eased back enough to swipe that tear with the pad of his thumb. Rubbing the moisture between his fingertips, Ian placed a kiss on her forehead.

"There are already towels out here in that bin beside the tub," he told her.

Ian started to pull away, but her eyes were wide, her mouth open, like she was still in shock.

"Did I say something wrong?" he asked.

Sara blinked and shook her head. "No, nothing's wrong."

She didn't move for a moment, like she was lost in a thought or in a trance. Ian snapped his fingers in front of her face and she jerked.

"Oh, sorry." She laughed again. "Everything is great, Ian. Let's check out this hot tub."

She immediately started stripping, hopping from one foot to the other.

"Damn, it's really cold out here," she stated.

Ian hurried out of his own clothes and climbed into the hot tub, then reached out his hand to assist her in. The moment Sara joined him, he wrapped her in his arms and they sank deeper into the warm water.

"This is the best way to end the day," she murmured against his lips. "How can I ever repay you for such an amazing gift?"

Ian's body stirred and he laughed. "You can show me your appreciation right now."

"He got me a freakin' hot tub and a redo of my back patio."

Elise and Delilah stared at her like she'd grown two heads.

"And he gave me a forehead kiss," Sara added.

"What the hell am I supposed to do now? How can I not fall for him?"

Sara smoothed her curls over her shoulder and really tried not to get worked up, but she couldn't help herself. She hadn't had a chance to tell her sisters and now they were getting ready to open the doors for the gala. But she needed advice and she needed…

She didn't even know what she needed at this point. All she could pinpoint with certainty was that she didn't want Ian to leave and she didn't know if she'd ever be able to get over him once he was gone.

"You're bringing this up now?" Elise demanded.

"I've been busy using the hot tub," Sara replied, smiling.

"We need to have a family meeting to talk about you and Ian. We're four minutes from opening the doors to our first Christmas at the Castle."

Delilah settled her hand on Sara's arm. "For what it's worth, I really like the guy."

Elise rolled her eyes. "He's great, okay? We tried to ruffle his feathers and he gave it right back to us. We can't help but think he's amazing, but if you're telling me you're in love because he kissed your forehead—"

"No, of course not," Sara groaned. "There are so many things that have made me feel this way and I just don't know what to do with all of these emotions."

"Of all the times for you to discover love." Elise

sighed. "Listen, we will talk and give you our best advice, but this will have to wait. I'm a nervous wreck that people won't show, I've been queasy all day because morning sickness clearly doesn't have a watch."

"I'm sorry." Guilt instantly replaced uncertainty and Sara reached for Elise's hand. "For what it's worth, you look stunning and Antonio is a lucky man."

Elise pulled in a deep breath and smiled. "Thanks. I won't be so cranky once I feel better. But I do like Ian, the little time I got to spend with him. And if you like him, if you *love* him, then he deserves to know before he leaves. Trust me on that one."

Yeah, if anyone knew what it was like to potentially lose a man to long distance, it was Elise. Antonio now divided his time between the US and Spain, but mostly spent it here with Elise. Sara figured he'd be here even more during this pregnancy so he could hover over her and make sure she wasn't overdoing it.

"Is Ian coming tonight?" Delilah asked.

Sara nodded. "He was still in town at Rise and Grind when I left the house. We decided to come separately since I had to be here early and he said he had a great idea for the opening to his book."

"A book?" Elise asked.

"He started his first chapter today." She couldn't believe the man could just sit down and spit out words like that. "That's his goal when he's done at the magazine, but we can discuss all of that later. Let's get this party started."

Sara had nerves, of course, because this was their first holiday party. Would people come? Would they be too busy because it was a chaotic time of year?

But the main source of her uneasiness came from not knowing how Ian would react to seeing her in her dress, how he would react when she opened up about her feelings or how he would react when she confessed she wanted to see where this relationship could go once he left. Maybe they could make this work. He didn't exactly act like he didn't want to be with her, but he'd also made it very clear he was leaving and moving on.

She couldn't just be a way to pass his time…she refused to believe that. He might hold his emotions close to his chest, but there was no way he'd be so giving and caring toward her if she was just a fling.

Then again, they'd never spent the night in her bed and they'd never had a meal at her dinner table. Everything was still casual, still very surface-level romance.

The large double doors opened at the same time and guests started milling in. The waitstaff in all black maneuvered fluidly through the crowd and Sara greeted people as she walked around. Her eyes never stopped scanning for Ian and she figured he'd show up in another of his suits with a vest. Somehow that look just fit him and made him stand out, when he so desperately wanted to hide in the shadows.

Sara lost track of time and how many people she chatted with and welcomed. Some familiar faces, some newcomers who wanted to check out the castle and likely some who wanted an incredible backdrop for their social media holiday pictures.

Across the open ballroom Elise stood by Antonio's side. He had his arm around her waist and they laughed at something another couple was saying. Sara scanned again and found Camden and Delilah, who were also chatting with customers Sara recognized. Her sisters had found their happily-ever-afters and Sara knew hers wasn't far…perhaps hers was in the making right now.

How could she know? How would she be certain when the right one for her came along?

She still didn't see Ian anywhere and Sara knew Rise and Grind had closed hours ago. Maybe he'd changed his mind. Perhaps a large gathering gave him pause and he just couldn't do it…even for her.

She couldn't make him someone he wasn't and she'd fallen for the man he was. But there was a huge part of her that wanted to save him. He lived with a pain she didn't understand and kept locked away and she just wanted to take all of that heartache and replace it with good memories.

If he didn't show, she'd understand, but she'd be disappointed. Regardless of what happened here, she planned on talking to him as soon as she got home. They both deserved for her to be honest about her feelings.

Seventeen

Breathtaking. Stunning. Flawless.

Ian could use so many words to describe Sara and yet none of them came close to capturing her essence.

He'd sneaked in nearly an hour ago and climbed the stairs to stand on the balcony that overlooked the ballroom. Guests came and went from the second story. Many up here were posing for pictures, he'd even been asked to take a few. But he sipped his bourbon and watched as Sara worked the room and did what she loved. This was her life, the smiling and mingling. Sara Hawthorne was a natural-born charmer. She loved being around people, she thrived in this atmosphere.

And he stood up here hiding.

It didn't matter how much he wanted to fit into her life, and even thinking that seemed absurd, but this was not where he belonged. She didn't know about him, not everything. She deserved someone who would stand by her side, just like her sisters' husbands. Sara would want a man she could be proud of.

They'd started this relationship in a bar. Who the hell meets their soul mate in a bar?

But Sara wasn't his soul mate. She was the woman who'd made him want to be a better man. She'd made him open his eyes to the life around him. She'd made him have fun, and he'd made some of the happiest memories of his life. He'd never forget her, but after tonight, he would be heading back to Miami. His flight left in the morning and no matter how many times he thought about moving it, he knew he couldn't keep putting off the inevitable.

Sara turned, the slight train of the red dress trailing behind her. He loved the sight of her bare, but seeing her in red had him doing a double take when he'd first spotted her. And from up here, he'd seen many men do the same. There was no denying she was a striking woman and he couldn't fault anyone for wanting another look.

She walked from one end of the ballroom to the other and happened to turn again…and she glanced up. Her gaze caught his and that wide smile came in an instant. So did the punch of lust that she continued to deliver with each glance.

Sara gathered the material of her skirt and started

up the curved steps. Ian gripped his tumbler and pushed off the railing to go meet her.

"How long have you been here?" she asked the moment she reached him. "I've been trying to watch for you."

"You were busy when I came in," he explained. "I've been admiring your beauty from up here. That dress…"

She held her arms wide and did a slow spin.

"You like?" she asked. "I was hoping you would."

The fact that she wondered how he would react to how she looked told him they were both far deeper into this relationship than he ever intended. Hell, he'd had no intentions, yet here they were.

Ian took her hands in his and stepped closer. "Other than in your hot tub the other night, you've never looked more beautiful."

She tipped her head and smiled as if him bringing that up in public embarrassed her. She sure as hell didn't seem embarrassed the other night.

"I'd like to talk to you," she told him. "I mean, not right here, but I have something I want to tell you."

That hope in her eyes had his gut tightening. He couldn't let her think there was something beyond this, and he had a feeling he was already too late.

"Sara—"

"We can talk when we get home."

Home. She said that word so calmly, as if they literally shared a home. But he'd never let himself fully invest himself into her place. He'd had to keep the distance wherever he could.

"My flight is tomorrow morning."

Her eyes widened and she took a slight step back as if he'd caught her off guard, and he likely had. He'd never told her for certain when he was leaving—he'd only said after the gala. But it was time, because the longer he stayed, the more difficult things would be when he actually left.

"I—I didn't realize," she murmured.

Ian waited for her to say more, but she pulled in a deep breath, squared her shoulders and tipped her chin. In an instant, she'd gone from shocked to strong and there wasn't a doubt in his mind that she was trying to hold it together.

"I didn't mean to spring that on you," he explained. "I had thought about moving it, but I'd like to get back before Christmas and I can't stay."

People moved around them. A server interrupted to see if they needed another drink or an appetizer. Nothing else mattered and there was nothing else Ian wanted except privacy. He hadn't meant to do this here and the last thing he wanted to do was hurt her. No matter when he left, there would be pain for both of them. In a short time, they'd come to mean something to each other. This was more than a fling and it was more than just a subject. But long-term wasn't in his plans and Sara deserved a man who could be everything she wanted and give her everything she deserved.

Sara continued to stare at him, but for the first time since meeting her, he couldn't get a bead on her thoughts—which likely meant she was doing a damn good job of masking this hurt.

"I need to see about our guests," she told him. "And check with the staff to see if they need anything."

So she was going to distance herself now. She was definitely hurt and he was a jerk for causing it. Unfortunately, there was no way around it. This was the reality they were dealt with.

When she started by him, Ian reached out and curled his fingers around the crook of her arm. She paused beside him, her gaze going from his loose grip to his eyes.

"What did you want to tell me?" he asked.

A corner of her mouth kicked up like she wanted to be happy, but the light had gone out.

"That I'm falling in love with you."

She held his gaze another moment before easing away from his touch.

"If you'll excuse me."

Sara left him standing there alone with that bomb she'd just dropped. He wasn't stupid or naive. He'd worried she was falling too fast, but hearing her say the words really gripped at his heart. She'd crossed over to another level that he could never be on.

How did he move on after this? More so, how could she be falling for him? They'd only known each other a few weeks.

Ian blew out a sigh and glanced up toward the

ceiling and exposed beams of the castle. And that's when he saw the mistletoe dangling. Wasn't that just ironic? Not kissing beneath the mistletoe had always been said to be bad luck.

Obviously, that wasn't a myth.

Sara stared at her cell, completely caught off guard at the number that had left a voice mail.

He'd called. Her father had called while she'd been at the gala and she'd just looked at her phone when she got back to her car.

She'd hoped Ian would have called or texted… anything, because she hadn't seen him again after they both dropped bold statements.

So there was that disappointment that Ian hadn't reached out, but she was also anxious that her father had. But what had he said? She was almost afraid to push Play. If he called to tell her he never wanted contact again, that would be it.

But surely he wouldn't have called if that was the case, right? He would have just ignored her and never reached out.

Sara adjusted the vents in her car and cranked up the heater, then she hit Play and waited for the familiar voice to come through her car speakers.

"Hi, Sara. Um, it's me. I can't stop thinking about you. My wife and I would like to meet with you. Whenever you're free, we'll make the drive. Call me when you can."

Tears instantly sprang into her eyes and she

glanced at the time. It was much too late to call him now, but she would tomorrow. After all of this time, she was finally going to meet the man who had been missing for her entire life.

She'd connected with her father on the same day the man she'd fallen in love with announced he was leaving town. Maybe that's just how fate wanted to help her heal. Maybe having her father in her life would help her move into the next chapter... the chapter without Ian.

Sara maneuvered through the curvy country roads and headed home. She replayed the message from her father the entire way. She would never get tired of hearing his voice and having him say he wanted to meet her.

When she pulled into her drive and up to the garage, her stomach tightened at the sight of Ian's vehicle. She'd thought he might get his stuff and hit a hotel for his flight tomorrow. She really hadn't known what to expect or if he'd be here when she got back. She wouldn't let her hopes get too high because they were already so low now. She couldn't mentally afford another letdown or more heartache.

She took her time gathering her dress and getting out of the car to head inside. She had no idea what to say or do at this point. Maybe he'd be asleep and she could slip into her room quietly. She really didn't know how she'd react or feel seeing him in private now that they were free to speak their minds. But if he was dead set on leaving, there was nothing she could say to make him stay.

Oh, she could plead her case and fight for what she wanted, but she didn't want to have to beg a man to be with her. She didn't want to make someone stay out of guilt or obligation.

Sara gripped her clutch and her cell and stepped into the utility room. She waited, but heard nothing. As she moved on into the kitchen, her eyes landed on Ian's laptop case and the suitcase at the island.

He'd packed, but he hadn't left. Yet.

The glow from her Christmas lights should be welcoming and heartwarming, but she wasn't feeling too festive right now.

She sat her clutch and phone on the island and gathered her skirt in one hand. Holding on to the edge of the counter, she slid off one heel and then the other, letting them clunk to the floor.

"I couldn't leave."

Sara jerked to see Ian in the arched doorway leading down the hallway. He still wore the black suit he'd had on at the gala, but his hair seemed quite a mess. Clearly he'd spent some time running his fingers through it and she had to admit, she was a little happy that he was just as frustrated.

"You weren't supposed to tell me you love me." His eyes remained down and he propped his hands on his narrow hips. "You weren't supposed to make me feel. I didn't want to feel."

Sara remained in place, saying nothing, because

he was obviously working through something all on his own and she had to let him.

"When my mother died, I swore I'd never get attached to anyone again," he went on, still staring down as if seeing something replaying before his eyes. "I see this damn scar on my face every day, the reminder I need that tells me I don't deserve someone else in my life."

Sara started to step toward him, but he held up his hand and met her gaze.

"No," he commanded. "Don't. You need to understand why I can't love you back."

He muttered a curse and then silence settled heavily in the room.

"I make a living out of stringing words together, but nothing is coming to me that sounds right. I'm out of my element here and it's terrifying."

As much as she wanted to say something, Sara nodded and let him continue. He had to work through his demons on his own before she could step in.

"I never knew my father," he started. "My mother was all I had. I loved her more than anything and I knew she'd do anything for me. When I became a teen, I guess I was like all teen boys and wanted to be a little rebellious to see what I could get away with. She would pull me back in and be stern, but loving."

Ian slid off his jacket, tossing it aside, then unbuttoned his cuffs and rolled his sleeves up his forearms. He raked his hands through his hair once more and blew out a sigh.

"We were arguing the day she died. The weather was horrible. Snowy and cold. I had just gotten my license and wanted to drive, but she kept insisting I wasn't ready. But I kept begging and she gave in. We started arguing when I slid the first time on a patch of ice. She wanted me to pull over and I told her I was fine, but then I slid again and…"

His voice cracked at that last word and Sara didn't try to refrain anymore. She took a step forward, then another, until she closed the gap between them.

She framed his face in her hands and swiped when a lone tear slid down right over his scar.

"That accident wasn't your fault," she insisted. "Deep in your heart you know that and I didn't know your mother, but I'm sure she wouldn't want you blaming yourself."

"She wouldn't," he whispered. "But that's not the issue here. I need you to know why I can't get close, why you can't love me, why I can't stay."

Oh, she understood perfectly.

"I needed to tell you all of that before I leave," he added. "I couldn't just go and have you wonder if there was something you did wrong because none of this is you. You're… Hell, Sara. You're everything."

Yes. Yes. Yes.

That's all she needed to hear, because that vulnerable statement was damn near a confession of love. The man just didn't know how to love or he was too afraid.

"Running from what we have won't make it go

away." She smoothed his wayward strands from his forehead. "You go back to Miami, and your thoughts and wants will still be with you. I will still be with you."

He closed his eyes and dropped his forehead to hers.

"This isn't how things were supposed to go," he admitted. "I thought I could handle this fling with you, but then I came here and you make me want a home. You make me want things I never thought I deserved."

"And why don't you?" she asked softly. "Because you're human and had an accident? You can't punish yourself for the rest of your life. That's just like if you had died that day. Don't you want to live? To make your mother even more proud than I'm sure she already is?"

"How do you do that?" he whispered.

Sara eased back, dropping her hands to take his.

"Make me feel like this is possible," he clarified.

"Because it is. If you want something, go for it." Sara swallowed her own fear and trudged on. "Do you want what we have, Ian? Do you want to see where this will go? Or do you want to continue hiding and letting life pass you by?"

He squeezed her hands and a blossom of hope filled her.

"You sound like Nigel," he said with a soft chuckle. "He's always telling me to live my life and stop watching life around me."

"He's a smart man."

Ian's damp eyes held hers and while her heart broke for him, she also had a piece that was so full of love and optimism. This could work, if only he would let it.

"You'd like him and his wife," Ian told her. "Maybe you can come to Miami and meet them sometime."

Sara smiled. "I'd like that."

"And maybe I could stay here. For now."

"I'd like that, too."

He continued to stare at her and she wondered what was going through his mind. All she knew was he was staying, he was giving them a chance, and there was no way they'd fail.

He ran his hands up and down her arms and then cupped her cheek. "When I talked to your sisters they said you'd been waiting for your own fairy tale, that you wanted that knight to come save the day."

Sara would have a talk with them about that later. "That's not exactly what I've said, but I do want a fairy tale."

"You have it." Ian's thumb raked over her bottom lip. "Only you didn't need saving, Sara. You were the one who saved me."

Sara's heart flipped and tears instantly sprang into her eyes. Never in her life had she thought she could save anyone. She'd wanted to fall in love with the right man and she wanted to have that companion forever, but she never thought she was strong enough to save someone's heart.

"I couldn't leave now if I wanted to," he added. "Because I'm falling in love with you, too."

Sara threw her arms around his neck and held tight. "I know you are. I just needed to hear you say it."

"I'll keep saying it, so long as you don't sing anymore."

A laugh escaped her and she pulled back enough to swat at his chest.

"That's rude, but I'll take that deal."

Ian's lips grazed over hers. "You can do anything you want, just promise you'll continue to be patient with me during this."

"I'm not going anywhere," she promised. "But I do have one request."

His brows drew in as he stared down at her. "Anything."

"My father called and wants to meet in person after the holidays." Just the thought had nerves dancing in her stomach. "Will you go with me?"

"I'll be right by your side."

Ian bent down and scooped her up into his arms and headed down the hallway.

"We're sleeping in your room from now on," he told her. "This is just the beginning of our own happily-ever-after."

Epilogue

Ian's hand settled around her waist as Sara snuggled deeper into his side. She couldn't help but smile as Delilah and Cam, Elise and Antonio all gathered in her living room. She'd decided to host a family Christmas Eve dinner and gift exchange. Though they'd all found love this year so what could be better than that?

"I hope someone got me a size seven-day cruise," Elise stated. "That fits me best."

"You just took a honeymoon," Delilah scolded, sitting on the arm of the sofa next to Cam.

Antonio shook his head as he swirled his bourbon. "She's turned into a travel fanatic. She's already in discussions with my mother about going to Spain after the first of the year."

Sara started to reply, but her doorbell rang. She glanced to Ian who had a sneaky smile on his face.

"What did you do?" she asked as she sat her wineglass on the accent table behind the sofa.

Ian merely shrugged. "Go find out."

Nerves curled in her belly, though she knew whatever Ian had done, he'd done out of love. She just couldn't fathom who else they were missing. Maybe he got a dog or perhaps a shipment of wine. She wouldn't be opposed to either of those gifts.

Sara reached the front door and pulled in a breath before turning the knob. But the moment she spotted her guest, Sara gasped. Her eyes immediately filled with tears, but she remained still.

"Merry Christmas."

Trenton Mills—her father—stood on her doorstep with a package in hand and a cautious smile on his face.

"I hope this is okay," he added.

Ian stepped up behind Sara and she turned to him. He offered her the widest grin.

"I thought this was better than anything I could purchase," he stated.

Sara glanced back to her father and laughed through the tears. "This is more than okay and absolutely the greatest gift."

Ian reached out for the package and gestured. "Come on in and welcome to the family."

Trenton held out his hand for Sara to shake and the moment her hand slid into his, the tears fell. He gave a gentle tug and she found herself fully embraced by the man she could now call father.

"We have so much to catch up on," he murmured in her ear. "This is just the beginning."

Yes. Just the beginning.

* * * * *

WE HOPE YOU ENJOYED
THIS BOOK FROM

H HARLEQUIN
DESIRE

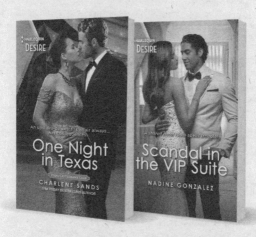

*Luxury, scandal, desire—welcome to
the lives of the American elite.*

Be transported to the worlds of oil barons, family dynasties,
moguls and celebrities. Get ready for juicy plot twists,
delicious sensuality and intriguing scandal.

6 NEW BOOKS AVAILABLE EVERY MONTH!

COMING NEXT MONTH FROM

HARLEQUIN
DESIRE

#2911 ONE CHRISTMAS NIGHT
Texas Cattleman's Club: Ranchers and Rivals
by Jules Bennett
Ryan Carter and Morgan Grandin usually fight like cats and dogs—until one fateful night at a Texas Cattleman's Club masquerade ball. Now will an unexpected pregnancy make these hot-and-heavy enemies permanent lovers?

#2912 MOST ELIGIBLE COWBOY
Devil's Bluffs • by Stacey Kennedy
Brokenhearted journalist Adeline Harlow is supposed to write an exposé on Colter Ward, Texas's Sexiest Bachelor, *not* fall into bed with him enthusiastically and repeatedly! If only it's enough to break their no-love-allowed rule for a second chance at happiness...

#2913 A VALENTINE FOR CHRISTMAS
Valentine Vineyards • by Reese Ryan
Prodigal son Julian Brandon begrudgingly returns home to fulfill a promise. Making peace with his troubled past and falling for sophisticated older woman Chandra Valentine aren't part of the plan. But what is it they say about best-laid plans...?

#2914 WORK-LOVE BALANCE
Blackwells of New York • by Nicki Night
When gorgeous TV producer Jordan Chambers offers Ivy Blackwell the chance of a lifetime, the celebrated heiress and social media influencer wonders if she can handle his tempting offer...and the passion that sizzles between them!

#2915 TWO RIVALS, ONE BED
The Eddington Heirs • by Zuri Day
Stakes can't get much higher for attorneys Maeve Eddington and Victor Cortez in the courtroom...or in the bedroom. With family fortunes on the line, these rivals will go to any lengths to win. But what if love is the ultimate prize?

#2916 BILLIONAIRE MAKEOVER
The Image Project • by Katherine Garbera
When PR whiz Olive Hayes transforms scruff CEO Dante Russo into the industry's sexiest bachelor, she realizes she's equally vulnerable to his charms. But is she falling for her new creation or the man underneath the makeover?

SPECIAL EXCERPT FROM

⟨H⟩HARLEQUIN

DESIRE

*Thanks to violinist Megan Han's one-night fling with her
father's new CFO, Daniel Pak, she's pregnant! No one
can know the truth—especially not her matchmaking
dad, who'd demand marriage. If only her commitment-
phobic not-so-ex lover would open his heart…*

Read on for a sneak peek at
One Night Only
by Jayci Lee.

The sway of Megan's hips mesmerized him as she glided
down the walkway ahead of him. He caught up with her
in three long strides and placed his hand on her lower
back. His nostrils flared as he caught a whiff of her sweet
floral scent, and reason slipped out of his mind.

He had been determined to keep his distance since
the night she came over to his place. He didn't want to
betray Mr. Han's trust further. And it wouldn't be easy
for Megan to keep another secret from her father. The
last thing he wanted was to add to her already full plate.
But when he saw her standing in the garden tonight—a
vision in her flowing red dress—he knew he would crawl
through burning coal to have her again.

She reached for his hand, and he threaded his fingers through hers, and she pulled them into a shadowy alcove and pressed her back against the wall. He placed his hands on either side of her head and stared at her face until his eyes adjusted to the dark. He sucked in a sharp breath when she slid her palms over his chest and wrapped her arms around his neck.

"I don't want to burden you with another secret to keep from your father." He held himself in check even as desire pumped through his veins.

"I think fighting this attraction between us is the bigger burden," she whispered. His head dipped toward her of its own volition, and she wet her lips. "What are you doing, Daniel?"

"Surviving," he said, his voice a low growl. "Because I can't live through another night without having you."

She smiled then—a sensual, triumphant smile—and he was lost.

Don't miss what happens next in…
One Night Only
by Jayci Lee.

Available December 2022 wherever
Harlequin Desire books and ebooks are sold.

Harlequin.com

Get 4 FREE REWARDS!

We'll send you 2 FREE Books plus 2 FREE Mystery Gifts.

FREE Value Over $20

Both the **Harlequin® Desire** and **Harlequin Presents®** series feature compelling novels filled with passion, sensuality and intriguing scandals.

YES! Please send me 2 FREE novels from the Harlequin Desire or Harlequin Presents series and my 2 FREE gifts (gifts are worth about $10 retail). After receiving them, if I don't wish to receive any more books, I can return the shipping statement marked "cancel." If I don't cancel, I will receive 6 brand-new Harlequin Presents Larger-Print books every month and be billed just $6.05 each in the U.S. or $6.24 each in Canada, a savings of at least 10% off the cover price or 6 Harlequin Desire books every month and be billed just $4.80 each in the U.S. or $5.49 each in Canada, a savings of at least 13% off the cover price. It's quite a bargain! Shipping and handling is just 50¢ per book in the U.S. and $1.25 per book in Canada.* I understand that accepting the 2 free books and gifts places me under no obligation to buy anything. I can always return a shipment and cancel at any time by calling the number below. The free books and gifts are mine to keep no matter what I decide.

Choose one: ☐ **Harlequin Desire**
(225/326 HDN GRTW)

☐ **Harlequin Presents Larger-Print**
(176/376 HDN GQ9Z)

Name (please print)

Address   Apt. #

City   State/Province   Zip/Postal Code

Email: Please check this box ☐ if you would like to receive newsletters and promotional emails from Harlequin Enterprises ULC and its affiliates. You can unsubscribe anytime.

Mail to the **Harlequin Reader Service:**
IN U.S.A.: P.O. Box 1341, Buffalo, NY 14240-8531
IN CANADA: P.O. Box 603, Fort Erie, Ontario L2A 5X3

Want to try 2 free books from another series! Call 1-800-873-8635 or visit www.ReaderService.com.

---

*Terms and prices subject to change without notice. Prices do not include sales taxes, which will be charged (if applicable) based on your state or country of residence. Canadian residents will be charged applicable taxes. Offer not valid in Quebec. This offer is limited to one order per household. Books received may not be as shown. Not valid for current subscribers to the Harlequin Presents or Harlequin Desire series. All orders subject to approval. Credit or debit balances in a customer's account(s) may be offset by any other outstanding balance owed by or to the customer. Please allow 4 to 6 weeks for delivery. Offer available while quantities last.

Your Privacy—Your information is being collected by Harlequin Enterprises ULC, operating as Harlequin Reader Service. For a complete summary of the information we collect, how we use this information and to whom it is disclosed, please visit our privacy notice located at corporate.harlequin.com/privacy-notice. From time to time we may also exchange your personal information with reputable third parties. If you wish to opt out of this sharing of your personal information, please visit readerservice.com/consumerschoice or call 1-800-873-8635. **Notice to California Residents**—Under California law, you have specific rights to control and access your data. For more information on these rights and how to exercise them, visit corporate.harlequin.com/california-privacy.

HDHP22R2

Love Harlequin romance?

DISCOVER.

Be the first to find out about promotions,
news and exclusive content!

f Facebook.com/HarlequinBooks

𝕐 Twitter.com/HarlequinBooks

◎ Instagram.com/HarlequinBooks

ⓟ Pinterest.com/HarlequinBooks

You Tube YouTube.com/HarlequinBooks

ReaderService.com

EXPLORE.

Sign up for the Harlequin e-newsletter and
download a free book from any series at
TryHarlequin.com

CONNECT.

Join our Harlequin community to
share your thoughts and connect
with other romance readers!
Facebook.com/groups/HarlequinConnection

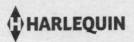

HARLEQUIN

Heartfelt or thrilling, passionate or uplifting—Harlequin is more than just happily-ever-after.

With twelve different series to choose from and new books available every month, you are sure to find stories that will move you, uplift you, inspire and delight you.

IF YOU ENJOYED THIS BOOK
WE THINK YOU WILL ALSO LOVE

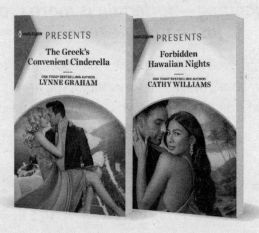

Escape to exotic locations where passion knows no bounds.

Welcome to the glamorous lives of royals and billionaires, where passion knows no bounds. Be swept into a world of luxury, wealth and exotic locations.

8 NEW BOOKS AVAILABLE EVERY MONTH!